HOLY WAR
ON AMERICAN SOIL!

It was a shocked public who woke to discover the terrible face of death staring back at them from their television sets—the bodies of twenty-nine men hung from the trees beyond the burned-out helicopters. It was a gruesome sight, but not nearly as frightening as the sight of the still-living victim nailed to a cross in the foreground. The SOCOM negotiator asked for the man's life—but the terror captain refused. . . .

Back in the swamp, Special Ops went silently to work. There was no talking. There was nothing to say. There were no rules, and the killing had just begun.

Berkley Books by James N. Pruitt

The SPECIAL OPERATIONS COMMAND Series

SPECIAL OPERATIONS COMMAND

#6

SWAMP KILL

JAMES N. PRUITT

B

BERKLEY BOOKS, NEW YORK

SPECIAL OPERATIONS COMMAND #6:
SWAMP KILL

A Berkley Book / published by arrangement with
the author

PRINTING HISTORY
Berkley edition / March 1992

ISBN: 0-425-13208-0

A BERKLEY BOOK ® TM 757,375
Berkley Books are published by The Berkley Publishing Group,
200 Madison Avenue, New York, New York 10016.
The name "BERKLEY" and the "B" logo
are trademarks belonging to Berkley Publishing Corporation.

PRINTED IN THE UNITED STATES OF AMERICA

10 9 8 7 6 5 4 3 2 1

CHAPTER 1

Major Juan Ruiz stood motionless on the wooden pier, watching the early-morning fog lift slowly from the surrounding waters of the Florida Everglades.

To either side of Ruiz, the khaki-clad guards remained impassive, their Soviet AK assault rifles slung over burly shoulders with an air of practiced casualness. They scanned the swamp waters with dead, gunmetal eyes that revealed no feeling or emotion. They had maintained their silent vigil for nearly an hour now, and thus they would remain throughout the day if Ruiz so ordered it.

There was an evil, unholy smell of death in these swamps. It seemed to hang in the gray mist that rose up out of the wet ground, and to drape itself from the long strands of Spanish moss that looped and curved around the trees. Even the trees themselves reeked of it; they were gaunt and stark, as if from another age, another world. Crowded together, each individual tree was nevertheless an entity, a symbol, a menace, with its long roots reaching out and searching to snatch any living thing from the still waters and damp earth that surrounded them.

The croaking frogs were constant and loud, as if they, too, were aware of the imminent evil.

There was no sun here. Somewhere out there, no doubt, the early-morning sun brightened a clearer sky. However, here, under the damp canopy of dark green and gray foliage, there was only the fog, the damp, and the cold. The heavy smell of rotting wood, humus, and decaying sludge permeated the air. It was a fearful, oppressive place, where nothing that was clean could ever live. Yet, here, in this hellhole, Major Juan Ruiz, a Cuban military advisor and commando par excellence, found himself sharing command of the world's most sought-after terrorist group. This group's combined skills and abilities had, over time, struck fear into the hearts of millions around the globe.

The terrorist force had begun arriving in a piecemeal fashion over the past two months. Major Ruiz, with six handpicked members of Castro's elite special warfare command, arrived first. They were responsible for locating and establishing a base of operations in this vast Florida wilderness. It was not an assignment that Juan Ruiz had requested. He was a soldier, not a terrorist. Neither he nor his men attacked helpless children aboard school buses, nor did they hijack airplanes or plant deadly bombs that indiscriminately killed men, women, and children. In the words of an international terrorist, "There are no innocents." He had questioned the assignment in Cuba. For all their bravado, bragging, and total disregard for human life, the terrorists were highly efficient in urban fighting, but practically ineffective in terrain such as that posed by the Florida Everglades. It was an environment in which Ruiz and his men were the experts. They would provide the edge that the terrorists would need to accomplish this rather strange mission in which Ruiz and his men now found themselves involved. They may have to help them, but they did not have to like them. Any idea that this feeling would change had disappeared with the arrival of the terrorists who had been handpicked for the assignment. There were only five of them in the first group, all Germans. They were members of the former Baader-Meinhof terrorist group that had ravaged Europe over the past decade. They were one of the earliest terrorist groups to be formed. Bombings, hijackings, assassinations, and kidnappings throughout Germany, Italy, and the Middle East had been attributed to the Baader-Meinhof gang. The reunification of East and West Germany had forced these remaining members of the terrorist group to seek sanctuary among other terrorist groups in the jungles of South America. Little had been heard of them since that time. The five Germans who arrived in Florida saw this as an opportunity to recapture past glories and serve notice to the world that the Baader-Meinhof group was still very much alive and still operational.

Their leader was a tall man named Kurt Mueller. He stood six foot four, with broad shoulders and massive arms. His blond hair and blue eyes personified Hitler's idea of the master race. The three other men with him were of equal size and build. Although he was younger, they were totally obedient to Mueller.

Much to Ruiz's dissatisfaction, the fifth member of this group was a woman. However, Eva Schmidt was every bit as dangerous and deadly as the men in whose company she traveled. She, too, was tall. She was a husky, big-boned woman, with short blond hair and steel-blue eyes that expressed that certain look of German superiority. In the two short weeks the Germans had been with the Cubans, there had been a number of minor confrontations, mostly instigated by Eva Schmidt. Ruiz had already classified the woman as a full-fledged psychopath and a total bitch who could easily entertain herself by spending hours twisting the heads off newborn babies. Ruiz quickly realized the complications that could arise and had secretly radioed a request that the Germans be removed from the operation. The request was denied.

Looking out over the fog-covered waters, Ruiz heard the sound of approaching footsteps moving onto the pier. He did not turn around. Ruiz glanced out of the corner of his eye at the guards who stood next to him. They had not heard the sound. *Pity,* he thought, *I hoped I had trained them better.*

The silence with which the visitor approached and the short steps he was taking gave away his identity. It could only be Ikia Imura, the Japanese leader of a group known as the Avenging Sun, a collection of radical Asians from Japan, Korea, and China, that had united to strike out against the Western world and its European allies for what they considered years of oppression and domination of the Asian race for Western profit and gain. Considered a renegade group in the terrorist world only a year ago, Imura and his followers had quickly earned respect among their peers following a well-planned and well-orchestrated attack on three separate airports in three different countries on the same day at exactly the same time. The death toll had been staggering: 123 people killed, another 200 wounded, and the destruction estimated in the millions. The cost to the Avenging Sun had been equally devastating. Imura lost 32 of his finest men and women in the attacks. Since that time, finding new recruits had been difficult. By participating in the defeat of the American leaders of the elite Special Operations Command, he would be assured a multitude of new recruits flocking to his cause. Imura and ten of his followers had arrived only a few days after the Germans. Like Mueller, Imura brought not one, but two women with him. These women, however, constituted no problem. Unlike the loudmouthed, cursing Eva Schmidt, the two young women with Imura observed the Oriental traditions of obedience and silence. Ruiz had yet to hear either of the women utter a single word since their arrival.

The stocky Japanese leader was only a few feet away when Ruiz, his eyes still scanning the swamp, asked, "Yes, Mr. Imura. Can I help you?"

The two Cuban guards turned suddenly, startled to find the Oriental standing within an arm's length of them both. The expressions on their faces were of shock and anger—anger at themselves that their perception of another presence on the pier had not been as keen as that of their commander.

Imura sighed as he raised his hands in a gesture of helplessness. "You are very good, Major. For a moment I felt I had the advantage."

Ruiz smiled as he cast a sidelong glance at Imura and said, "A moment of overconfidence has been known to get one killed, my friend."

Imura nodded curtly, his eyes flickering rapidly from one of the guards to the other, signaling that if this had been a real situation, without Ruiz's presence, he could have easily killed both of them. The message did not go unnoticed by the two Cubans, who nodded in appreciation of the lesson. Turning his gaze back to Ruiz, Imura asked, "Still no sign of our leader, Ahmad Fisal, and his men? Do you think he could have had trouble?"

Ruiz watched the early-morning fog slowly creeping through the cypress trees as he replied, "No, Fisal is a man of caution. He is also a man of patience, and would not risk the mission in order to maintain a time schedule. The twenty members of the PLO he was to rendezvous with last night constitute the largest contingent of our forces. It would be reasonable to assume that moving such a large number secretly through this wasteland would be cause for unexpected delays."

As if on cue, the burly guard to Ruiz's right stiffened, craning slightly forward toward the water with his head turned and one ear cocked, listening. After a few seconds, the guard turned to nod to Ruiz.

"They come," the guard said simply and without expression. Ruiz nodded in response, pleased that the Imura incident had sharpened their senses. He had heard them approaching at the same instant. Imura squinted his eyes and turned his ear to the fog. He heard nothing from the placid waters. A dark hastening speck appeared amid the lifting mist, gradually growing and taking shape until Ruiz recognized the outline of the swamp boat.

Five other dugouts laden with armed men suddenly appeared to the left and the right of the head craft. The narrow boats were cutting silent ripples through the water. A man in the stern of each with a long pole punted them along. The tree moss hung down to the water, and from time to time the dugouts disappeared into the lush greenery, reappearing again in menacing silence—always in silence—a little closer.

Standing in the prow of the lead boat, Ahmad Fisal pointed toward the faint outline of the dock and the figures awaiting his arrival. "There—to the right. Do you see the dock?" The pole man nodded. Pulling his stick from the water, he swung it out to the left and back into the water without a sound, pushing the dugout in its new direction.

The rich smell of the swamp was sulfuric, the smell of rotting eggs. Fisal hated the swamp, the stench, the damp, and the loneliness of it all, but he had taken the oath that all dedicated to the Palestinian cause had taken. This was his home now. His home for as long as the mission would last.

The cold dampness of this place brought nightly pain to his scarred right leg. It was an old wound and caused him to limp badly. Two Israeli bullets, years ago when he was a youth, had crippled him, and he had never forgiven them for that. True, at the time he was shot, he and other youths were stoning Israeli worshipers at their holy place. But in his eyes it was only right, it was land that had been stolen from the Palestinians. He had quickly learned that stones were no match for bullets, and now the PLO was his life. He reveled in its hatreds, its violence, and in its dreadful, distorted sense of power. Fisal took a kind of masochistic pleasure in suffering the miseries of this place for the cause.

The fog began to dissipate as Fisal's dugout drew nearer the pier. Ruiz could now distinguish features of the Arab leader's face. Once, perhaps, Fisal had been handsome, but now his face was too hard, too cruel for good looks. There were deep lines at the sides of his mouth, and a bitter, sardonic glint in his eyes. Ahmad Fisal was a man filled with hatred, which was surpassed only by his dislike for Americans, who he saw as the driving force behind the Jewish state that had stolen his homeland.

Ruiz motioned for the guards to assist Fisal and his men onto the dock and to secure their boats. Imura bowed slightly at the waist as the Arab leader stepped onto the wooden planking. Fisal ignored the gesture. Turning to observe the remaining dugouts as they approached, he yelled for them to hurry up.

"Did you have any problems?" asked Ruiz, while allowing his eyes to evaluate some of the new arrivals who stood to either side of Fisal. They were as tall, or taller than Fisal. Some had beards or mustaches or both. Ruiz noted the one similarity they all shared—the look of cruelty and hatred in their faces and the continuous shifting of their threatening eyes gleaming with suspicion. They all carried Russian AK-47s.

Fisal did not bother to look at Ruiz. Locking his hands behind his back, he answered in his usual cold and distant tone, "Only a minor problem. This morning four American youths were airboating through the saw grass along our route. Unfortunately, they observed some of our men and their weapons."

Momentary panic seized Ruiz. He and his men had labored two long, hard months in this sweltering muck and endured trying living conditions in careful preparation for this daring operation. The work had been completed in total secrecy and without incident. The thought of compromise now that they were ready to put their plan into operation justified the Cuban officer's concern. Struggling to control the emotion in his voice, Ruiz glanced at Imura, who seemed equally worried. Then he asked, "If they saw the weapons, they would surely report the sighting to the authorities."

Fisal, his hands still locked behind his back, rocked on his heels as he answered, "Have no fear, Major; our mission has not been compromised."

Imura started to step toward Fisal. Two of the PLO men brought their rifles up in a threatening manner. Their leader had not called for the Japanese man to approach. Imura showed his distaste, but stepped back and said, "The major is correct. They will report our—"

Fisal brought his hand up, cutting off Imura. "No. They will not!"

"How can you be sure?" asked Ruiz.

Fisal turned to face the two concerned men. His eyes met theirs and with a smug grin he pointed to the final dugout emerging from the lifting fog. "Is that assurance enough for you, gentlemen?"

Ruiz and Imura glanced at one another briefly, then at the four captives, three young men and a girl. Their wrists were tightly bound behind their backs. The long rope joined them, cutting into their necks, drawing blood with its chafing. They had been beaten, all of them, even the girl. There was a lost, bewildered expression on her childlike face. She was scared beyond belief, not understanding in the least what she and the others had done to bring on this nightmare.

The dugout was secured to the dock, and the prisoners unceremoniously jerked up and tossed roughly onto the pier. Ruiz was about to question the reason for bringing the prisoners to their base camp when Kurt Mueller and his mistress arrived. "Ah, I see the fishing was good today, Ahmad," said the big German.

Eva, spying the attractive young woman, walked past the men and knelt down beside the frightened girl. Eva studied her long, beautiful legs that ran up to tight shorts, then traveled to the dirt-stained blouse that covered small but firm young breasts with nipples that showed through the wet material. The girl's hair was corn-yellow. Her deep blue eyes showed the fear that was racing through her beautiful body. Reaching her hand out, Eva stroked the girl's ruffled hair, allowing her hand to move down to the soft, well-tanned, tearstained cheek. "So beautiful," she whispered. "So soft."

For a fleeting moment the terrified girl experienced a flickering of hope, a sense of security now that she was not the only female among this circle of frightening men with guns. However, that illusion of safety was suddenly shattered as the older woman's hand roamed down her neck and roughly cupped one of the girl's breasts tightly in her grip. The girl screamed and jerked away, her voice pleading,

"No! No, please—for God's sake, stop this. We haven't done anything wrong. Who—who are you people?"

The girl's rejection of Eva's advances sent the woman into a rage. Reaching out, she grabbed a handful of blond hair, jerking the girl forward and slapping her a vicious blow as she screamed, "Stop your whining, you American bitch."

The young man tied behind the girl looked up. His dark, angry eyes were glazed over. His fear and confusion evident, he muttered, "My God, this is America. You—you people can't do this—this can't happen here."

One of the PLO men stepped forward and yanked on the neck-rope, turning the boy's face up to him. "You are wrong, Yankee dog!" he said as he drove a powerful fist straight down into the boy's face. A sickening sound signaled that the blow had broken the boy's nose. Blood began to pour freely down the front of his shirt as he slumped back, unconscious. The sight of blood seemed to send the PLO men into a frenzy as they began beating and kicking the other two boys.

"Enough!" yelled Ruiz, as he stepped forward, grabbing Eva's uplifted hand before she could slap the crying young girl again. "Dammit, Fisal, call off your dogs."

Fisal had only to flip his wrist to get the Palestinians to move away from the bleeding, battered teenagers. Raising a questioning eyebrow, Fisal stared at Ruiz. "If the sight of blood bothers you, Major, perhaps you are in the wrong business."

Forcing Eva Schmidt to her feet, the major flung her roughly toward Mueller, then turned back to face Fisal. "I am a soldier. I have seen my share of blood, Fisal, but I will not stand by and watch men who I am to fight beside act like a pack of crazed animals. We have a job to do here. I suggest we set about doing that job, rather than beating on a helpless group of children."

Fisal stood still for a long moment, eyeing the Cuban officer. Nodding in agreement, he said, "Of course, you are right. We must not let this source of entertainment distract us from our main purpose." Motioning to three of his men, he continued, "Take these infidels to the base camp and tie them to a tree. I will decide their fate later."

Pulling the prisoners to their feet, the PLO followers led them off the pier and up the trail toward the well-hidden base camp, which was skillfully constructed among the thick cypresses and towering royal palms. One of the youths looked back at Fisal and shouted, "You're not going to get away with this. You know that, don't you? When we don't return by tonight, they will begin a search for us by tomorrow morning. Then you'll get yours, you fuckin' rag-head!"

One of the guards reached out and hit the youth in the face with the butt of his rifle, knocking him to the ground; the rope around his neck painfully pulled the others down with him. Cursing and kicking at the foursome, the guards got them back on their feet and marched them away.

"He is right, you know," said Imura. "Their families will be in a panic by morning. The authorities will begin a search by first light tomorrow. You can count on it."

"What about their airboat?" asked Ruiz.

"We towed it into the swamp with us. It was dismantled along the way here and the pieces sunk at various points. No one will ever find it," said Fisal. "I estimate it will be two, maybe three days before they widen their search this far into the swamps. Our mission against the Special Operations Command will begin within twenty-four hours. Once we have made our strike, the attention of the authorities, as well as the attention of the world, will be focused on us and the men of SOCOM as we begin our little game. The fate of those four will be quickly forgotten, I assure you. Now, come, let us see to the new arrivals, then go over our plan one last time."

They all agreed. Walking up the trail, Eva Schmidt hesitated. Dropping back, she fell in beside Ruiz and whispered, "Do not ever put your hands on me again—unless, of course, I want you to. Next time, I will kill you."

Ruiz stopped in the middle of the trail and stared at the husky woman as she continued up the trail to join Mueller. Imura paused next to Ruiz and watched as the others rounded a bend in the trail and disappeared from sight before he said, "I have never encountered a woman who harbored so much evil within her as that one. You would be wise not to turn your back on her, my friend. She is like the black widow—once she has mated, she kills and devours her lover."

The thought of being Eva's lover sent a chill down the Cuban's back. As he began to walk again, he replied, "What you say is true, Imura, but the only mating that bitch will ever get from me will come when I make her wrap her lips around the barrel of my pistol before I blow her brains out."

Imura chuckled as they rounded the bend. "With this one, Major, such action may be unwise. I believe a woman of her experience could possibly suck the bullets from your gun before you fired."

Both men were laughing as they crossed the small clearing beneath a canopy of cypress trees that led to the thatched hut of Ahmad Fisal.

Captain Ramon Garcia, the major's second-in-command, was already seated at the large, makeshift table that had been constructed of mangrove limbs and vines. Mueller and the bitch sat to his right. Takeo Ohira, a Korean, and

Imura's lieutenant, sat on the left. An empty chair was next to him for Imura. Fisal sat at one end of the table. Three Palestinians stood behind him with their faces void of expression and their rifles cradled across their bodies. The vacant chair at the other end of the table was for Ruiz. For men who were supposedly united for a common cause, Ruiz sensed an air of hostility in the crowded confines of Fisal's quarters. Allowing Ruiz time to be seated, Fisal clasped his hands in front of him, cleared his throat, then began. "With the arrival of my Palestinian brothers, I believe we are at last ready to begin our task. Their addition to our forces provides us with a total strength of forty-four. Surely, that should be more than sufficient for the elimination of six men of the Special Operations Command. Do you not agree, Major Ruiz?"

Ruiz lit a cigarette. Forcing a puff of smoke out of his nose, he replied, "Yes, I would think that would provide us with the necessary edge against such men as these."

Eva Schmidt broke out in mocking laughter. "My God, that is seven-to-one odds, and he 'thinks' that should be enough. What would you prefer, Major? Ten-to-one? Maybe twenty-to-one is more to your liking. This is ridiculous! They are only six men, Major Ruiz. You talk as if they were some type of supermen."

Both Fisal and Imura stared intently at the woman. In their countries such interruptions, let alone such arrogance, would not be tolerated. "Herr Mueller," said Fisal, his voice low and tight, "you will control your woman or I shall see to it that she is removed from this meeting."

Mueller stared around the table at the hostile looks he was receiving from the others. He didn't care. There was a defiant independence in his rough tone as he said, "Fräulein Schmidt has been with our organization for over ten years. She is my second in this matter and has risked her life on

numerous occasions, just as we all have. Therefore, she has
equal status in the discussions at this table. Now that we
have that settled, would you care to answer the lady's
question, Major? For you see, I, too, feel we are taking the
arrival of six Americans a little too seriously. As a matter of
fact, I fail to see how this will prove to be any contest at
all."

There was a moment of awkward silence as Ruiz took a
slow puff of his cigarette, exhaled it slowly, and looked
at Mueller. "It is apparent that neither you nor Miss
Schmidt have bothered to go over the collective intelligence. Is that correct, Herr Mueller?"

Mueller spoke up suddenly, his voice stern, "What
is there to read, Ruiz? You gather us here in this—this
pesthole, construct an elaborate plan to lure six Americans
into these swamps, and for what? Merely to kill them! A
task that could easily be accomplished on any street corner
in the city of Tampa Bay—but no, Castro and Abu Abbas
want to humiliate the Americans in the eyes of the world.
Okay, so be it. We get them in here while the world waits
and watches to see who wins this rather ridiculous game,
and we kill them. They are still only six men, Major Ruiz."

Ruiz shook his head in disgust and leaned back against a
pole of the hut. He had always heard of how meticulous
Germans were at everything they did. Apparently, Mueller
was not a full-blooded German—more like a cross between
an idiot and a total asshole. His ranting speech had just
demonstrated both of these qualities abundantly.

Fisal opened one of the folders that lay in front of him
and began to read. "General Jonathan J. Johnson, age sixty.
Twenty-nine years of service. Graduate of West Point. One
of the few remaining members of the old Army Air Corps.
Became Air Force officer when Army dropped Air Corps.
Personally selected by the president of the United States to

head the Special Operations Command. Combat experience: three tours of Vietnam as a combat fighter pilot, shot down twice, captured once, held for three months; escaped. Survived for one month on his own before rescue. Has strong links with the CIA and has, even now, on occasion, been involved in combat actions in support of his command. He is highly respected by his men and has a considerable following among important members of the Congress and Senate in Washington."

Mueller's curiosity began to get the better of him. Ruiz had been correct. He had not read the folders they had been provided on their arrival. The Everglades, for all its faults, seemed to serve as a sexual stimulus for the vigorous Eva. Her continued demands on him had precluded anything but sex and sleep since their arrival. Captain Garcia, noticing the change in the German's eyes, slid his folders down the table to the stern-faced Mueller, who opened the one tabbed with General Johnson's name at the top and began to read along as Fisal outlined the general's movements over the past forty-eight hours.

Fisal, having paused for a moment, continued. "Sources confirm that General Johnson, as well as our other two primary targets, will be the guest speaker at a joint dedication and Special Operations unit party scheduled for the day after tomorrow in the Gadsden Point National Recreational Area."

Mueller looked up from the file just as Garcia began reading from the second file. Pushing the Johnson file in front of Eva and nodding for her to read it, he quickly opened the second file and followed along.

"Major Bobby Joe Mattson. Born in West Texas. Age forty-three. Eighteen years of service. Extensive Special Warfare background. Has seen action in Vietnam, Laos, Cambodia, Central and South America, as well as two years in the Middle East. The major has a multitude of military skills. In Vietnam, he was an enlisted man and served as a Green Beret medic. He was wounded while serving as a member of a long-range recon team. Following a break in service, he returned to the military with a degree from Texas A&M and the rank of lieutenant. He is an expert in light and heavy weapons, explosives, communications, and especially, intelligence. He is parachute and scuba qualified and is a student of Tae Kwon Do—present rating, black belt. He was selected by General Johnson as his chief problem-handler and observer for highly sensitive missions. He is married and has two children. He and his wife have just reconciled following an eighteen-month separation. The major is scheduled to be promoted to the rank of colonel at the festivities the day after tomorrow." Garcia closed the file and leaned back in his chair.

Imura looked up from his file as he asked, "Do you not mean lieutenant colonel, Captain Garcia?"

"No, Mr. Imura. You are correct, however. That should be the next step in the American military system; however, Major Mattson's exceptional performance over the past eighteen months has endeared the man to the president, as well as the members of the Armed Services Committee. They feel Major Mattson has displayed exceptional leadership qualities in his handling of some rather difficult situations. Especially this last affair, which has gained not only Mattson, but the entire unit, national recognition. That, I might add, is the chief reason we are here. Under the guidance of General Johnson, SOCOM's last five missions have been a total success, thanks largely to the effectiveness of Mattson and his associate, Lieutenant Commander Mortimer. This success has not only brought these men notoriety in America, but worldwide recognition as well."

Imura slowly nodded as he said, "Ah, yes; the unfortunate incident involving Cuba and the selling of some chemicals he discovered off his coast. That was certainly a great loss to our Arab allies."

Eva Schmidt could not allow the opportunity to humiliate the Cuban, Ruiz, and the Arab leader, Fisal, to pass without comment. Smiling her crude smile, and with a hint of sarcasm in her voice, she said, "Yes, Mr. Imura, it was a loss that now has a number of Cubans, as well as Arabs, wondering if perhaps it is not time for a change in leadership." She hesitated long enough to let her eyes come to rest on Fisal, then continued. "Such rumors have, and justifiably so, become a major concern to Fidel and the PLO leadership. SOCOM's continued success has made a laughingstock of the word 'terrorist.' This last affair involving our Cuban and Arab friends served only to add to that laughter. Isn't that correct, Major Ruiz?"

Ruiz leaned forward. Resting his forearms on the edge of the table, he removed the stub of a cigarette from his lips and crushed it out in the palm of his left hand. He was not a masochistic man who found pleasure in self-induced pain. It was merely to regain self-control; otherwise, he might reach across the table and slap the hell out of the smug bitch. Wiping the ashes from his hand, the major chose to ignore her question. Eva Schmidt displayed a self-satisfied smile as she watched Ruiz open the third and final file without answering.

"Our third target for elimination is Lieutenant Commander Jacob Winfield Mortimer, United States Navy. Age thirty-two. Handpicked by General Johnson to serve as Major Mattson's partner in the field. If you read the file, you will see that the commander is a unique character and possibly the most dangerous of the trio. I say that due to the background information we have available. I believe you will find that information as intriguing as I did. A thirty-two-year-old bachelor from a wealthy Philadelphia family with a law degree from Harvard and a bank account that contains more money than any of us at this table will ever see. Yet he is a mere commander in the Navy. What does that tell you?"

Mueller laughed. "That he is an idiot."

"Hardly," replied Ruiz. "You will note that he attended the U.S. Naval Academy at Annapolis, graduating at the head of his class. Here again, it is interesting that he attained only the rank of the other cadets. No special considerations; no family influences or special treatment were requested nor given."

"I see also that he is a Navy SEAL," said Imura, "not one to choose the easy path, it would appear."

"That is correct," said Ruiz. "In the past, the commander has served as the leader of a specially designated SEAL team attached to the famed Delta Force, America's top antiterrorist unit. It was this same Navy commander who was effective in halting Libya's attempted takeover of Chad through the use of mercenaries last year. The man is skilled in a variety of weapons and, like his partner, Major Mattson, holds a black belt in Tae Kwon Do."

"Huh!" grunted Mueller. "So he is a rich bastard who can do tricks with his feet! That is supposed to make him a dangerous man?"

"No, Herr Mueller," replied Fisal wearily, disappointed that the German failed to see the significance of Major Ruiz's evaluation. "The fact that this man has none of the normal needs or financial desires that other men seek is what makes Commander Mortimer dangerous. Here is a man who could go anywhere, be anything he wanted, do whatever he liked, whenever he chose; yet, with all these options available to him, he forsakes these luxuries in order to maintain a lowly station in life as a Navy commander in his country's service, and he likes it, Herr Mueller. Privileges and riches cannot challenge one's inner self, cannot test one's inner strengths and weaknesses. The determination to seek out those challenges and constantly perform those tests upon himself is what makes this man dangerous, my friend. Very dangerous, indeed."

"This man has no weaknesses?" asked Eva.

"Only one," said Garcia. "Women. He is reported to be quite the ladies' man."

The husky German woman showed her first true interest in the meeting as she straightened in her chair and opened the file in front of her. "Oh, really. That could prove very useful to me later on," she said in a sultry voice.

Garcia cast a sideways glance at Ruiz and grinned. He wasn't sure if his commander would approve of what he was about to say, but the bitch had left herself open for a cutting remark. Looking back at Eva Schmidt, the Cuban leaned back in his chair, and with a casual bluntness said, "I'm sorry, Miss Schmidt, but I'm afraid the commander prefers attractive, well-built women over Amazons who look as though they practice sumo wrestling—no offense, Mr. Imura," said Garcia, nodding to the smiling Japanese at the table.

Eva Schmidt's head shot up, her eyes ablaze with anger, her mouth open to unleash a barrage at the young Cuban officer.

Fisal never gave her the chance. A pistol had suddenly appeared in the Arab's hand. He banged it heavily down onto the tabletop. "Enough of this! Do not speak, woman! You will keep your mouth shut and listen, or I swear by Allah, I shall blow your brains all over this room."

The grin on Garcia's face suddenly vanished, as did Imura's laughter. There was no smile on Ruiz's face as he watched the three PLO men behind Fisal level their AKs at the people around the table. Fisal allowed his stare to linger a moment on each individual as he spoke.

"It is apparent that few present at this table take our mission here seriously, but that attitude will change, and it will change quickly. I will no longer tolerate petty bickering and constant interruptions. A great deal of time and expense have gone into this operation. For it to be jeopardized from within is not acceptable. We will succeed in restoring the power of fear we once held over the world, with or without your assistance. My Palestinian brothers and I shall accomplish this mission alone, if necessary."

Fisal grabbed up the pistol. His voice rose and his face flushed red with anger. The pistol shook momentarily in his hand, the barrel pointed toward the roof. Realizing he was losing his grip on the situation, Fisal steadied his hand, inhaled deeply, and lowered the pistol back to the table. Regaining his composure and calming his tone considerably, he glanced around the group without singling out any one person and said, "You—you see what effect your petty arguments have on me. I warn you, for your own good, put these silly quarrels aside. We must be united to succeed in our quest."

A tense silence hung over the room as the others sat perfectly still, staring down the barrels of the rifles still pointed at them. They knew Fisal needed only to flick his finger and they would be shot to pieces. Eva Schmidt became an instant believer in that possibility.

Fisal rubbed his tired eyes. Replacing the pistol into his holster, he stood, and waving for the men with rifles to leave, he turned back to the group. "Perhaps we are all tired. It has been a long night for me and the others. Think seriously of what I have said. United, there is no one who can defeat us. Major Ruiz, wake me in a few hours. I want to go over our plan with those who are leaving tonight to begin the first phase of the operation."

"Mr. Fisal, sir," said Garcia quickly, "what about the four prisoners?"

The Arab ran his fingers along his wrinkled brow for a moment before replying. "See that they are fed and given water. I will decide what to do with them later. Now, if you will all excuse me, I really must get some sleep."

Ruiz and the others stood, and taking their folders with them, left the hut. Walking across the small makeshift compound, Eva began to taunt Garcia about the young female captive tied to the tree. "Do you think that young woman with the firm breasts would meet with Commander Mortimer's approval, Captain Garcia? Maybe you should sample it for him first. Is that what you have in mind, Garcia? Dipping your pathetic, little wick into the poor, frightened girl."

Garcia reached out to grab the woman. Ruiz caught the officer's arm and pushed him away. "Let it go, Garcia! See to it the prisoners are fed as you were ordered. Make sure you check their bindings as well. Now, go!"

Garcia turned and walked away in silence. His fists were tightly clenched. Turning back to Mueller, Ruiz said, "Have you already forgotten the lesson of only a few moments ago? The man in that hut was within a hair's breadth of killing us all. If you had dealt more with the Arab terrorists as did your predecessors who formed your group, you would realize that." Looking to Eva, Ruiz added, "This woman and her mouth are going to get you killed one day. You have been warned."

Eva Schmidt was about to say something as the Cuban turned and walked away. Mueller signaled with his hand for her to remain silent. She complied. Waiting until Ruiz was out of sight, she laughed under her breath, then placed her hand on Mueller's broad back and began to rub gently as she said, "Kurt, my love, it would appear that we are by far the superior group involved in this little game. How much longer do you intend to endure their insulting remarks and petty threats?"

Cupping one of her oversized breasts in his hand, Mueller smiled as he roughly squeezed the soft globe. "Not much longer, my sharp-tongued pet. You must exercise more patience, Eva. Our time will come."

Nuzzling up to Mueller, the woman ran her hand down to his groin and cupped her hand between his legs. Licking his ear, she whispered, "Exercise sounds like a perfect idea."

CHAPTER 2

Day 1
Tampa Airport

B. J. Mattson finished his glass of beer. Looking up at the television monitor that listed the arrival schedules for American Airlines, he saw that nothing had changed in the past thirty seconds since he had last checked the screen.

"Jesus, B.J.," laughed Jake Mortimer, "you're going to have a permanent neck injury if you keep staring at that damn monitor. Relax. We've still got thirty minutes before Charlotte and the kids arrive. You want another beer?"

Mattson glanced over at his partner, nodded, and said, "Yeah, but it's my turn to buy." Waving to the bartender for two more draft beers, Mattson leaned back in the cushioned chair in the Tampa Bay Airport bar. Jake was right. He was nervous; but then, Charlotte and the kids had been gone for over a year. The separation hadn't been easy on anyone. You didn't take almost twenty years of marriage and hang it out to dry and hope the old spark would still be there eighteen months later, without being worried. Charlotte had called him as soon as the story had broken about SOCOM's last mission. As usual, CNN had the right people in the right places at the right time. Major B. J. Mattson and Lieutenant Jacob Winfield Mortimer IV had suddenly found themselves on worldwide television. The normal security procedures and hush-hush activities of SOCOM had been abandoned at the request of the president. America needed its heroes. It was felt the exposure would not only be good for the country, but would also serve to send a clear message to those who would plot against the United States and her allies, that such actions would bring an effective and rapid response from America's elite Special Operations Command.

CNN had done an in-depth analysis of SOCOM, its functions and its personnel. There had been interviews with General J. J. Johnson, whose snow-white hair and down-home attitudes and speech immediately endeared him to millions across the country. The leathery but kind face of the unit commander had made the cover of *Time* and *Newsweek*. SOCOM became an overnight success, and the people of America loved it.

It had been these in-depth interviews with various officials and leaders in Washington that had made Charlotte Mattson realize the scope of responsibility that had been thrust upon her husband. In all the time they had been stationed at MacDill Air Force Base in Tampa, B.J. had done nothing but minimize his duties and importance as a member of SOCOM. He hadn't wanted her to worry, and for the first time she understood the motivation behind her husband's desire to continue his work in the military. They had talked for over two hours on the phone. By the time the conversation had ended, the problems had been resolved, and she was finally coming home where she belonged.

"Uh oh," whispered Jake, nodding toward the TV behind the bar. A CNN reporter was standing in a hallway outside a congressional meeting room. Behind her, a sign on the double doors read "Closed hearings in progress."

. "Wonder how our boy, General Sweet, and the Navy boys are holding up in that inquiry?" said Jake.

B.J. shook his head slowly as he replied, "Anybody's guess, partner. I feel kind of sorry for that admiral who Sweet conned into stopping that Iraqi ship in international waters off Cuba. Hell, he didn't know Sweet was only out to show us up."

"Yeah," said Jake as he lifted his beer. "That's one admiral who will be retiring real soon, no matter what the outcome of that investigation." Both men turned their attention to the screen as the attractive reporter from CNN began her story.

"Sources close to the investigation into the charges that the American Navy violated international law by firing shots across the bow of an Iraqi ship and then illegally boarded that vessel under arms, have said that there will be a number of reprimands forthcoming, and that certain high-echelon personnel will be asked to resign by the end of the day. Rumors still persist that the focus of these closed-door investigations is somehow linked to the successful counterterrorist actions taken by members of the elite Special Operations Command. The two leaders of that operation were Major B. J. Mattson and Navy Lieutenant Commander Jacob Mortimer, seen here as they were filmed returning from their mission with a number of Castro's Cuban officers and men who had aided them in the operation. Mattson and Mortimer have offered no comment on the current hearings."

"Not real photogenic, are you, B.J.?" laughed Jake as the two officers watched themselves stepping out of the Cuban PT boats with Joaquin Ochoa and his men. It was the same piece of film that had been run by every major news network around the world following the announcement of the successful completion of the operation. B.J. and Jake had become overnight heroes.

The cameras were back on the reporter now. "Inquiries by CNN as to why an Army general assigned to SOCOM has spent two complete days testifying before this committee has garnered little more than a 'no comment' from General J. J. Johnson, the commander of SOCOM. In a time when the once secretive unit has finally gone public, it would seem there are still a number of secrets that even SOCOM does not care to have aired publicly. From Washington, this is Beverly Mills, CNN News."

"Not a bad looking gal, Jake," said B.J. "How many times you been out with her now?"

"Seven," smiled Jake. "She stays on the go most of the time. Real sharp woman. She's going to head her own news staff one of these days if she keeps going like she is."

"Anything serious between you two?"

"Naw, she was just kind of fascinated by all the high-speed James Bond type of stuff we do—you know. Kind of like a SOCOM groupie. But, I've got to admit, she had the old adrenaline pumping."

"Boy, that's a relief. For a minute there I thought you were going to say that she was fascinated by those baby-blues of yours and that overpowering, Navy SEAL charm," grinned B.J.

"Well, that could have had a lot to do with it."

"Naw," laughed Mattson. "You just said she was smart. If that were the case, it would be a contradiction in terms."

"Screw you, Mattson," retorted Jake.

Mattson stood up. Tossing some money on the bar, he made a limp-wrist motion which drew the attention of a few others at the bar. Puckering up his lips, he smacked them at Jake and said, loud enough for all to hear, "I'm sorry, sailor, but I've decided to go back to my wife." Swinging his hips in a feminine fashion, Mattson walked out of the bar leaving a red-faced Jake feeling the stares of everyone in the room.

Quickly standing, Jake went after B.J. As he was about to go out the door of the bar, a blond man sitting near the door winked playfully at Jake and whispered, "If you can't change his mind, come back."

"Hey, buddy, fuck off!" said Jake as he opened the door, whispering under his breath, "Mattson, you asshole."

Jake caught up with B.J. at the waiting area. The passengers were just exiting the aircraft. Mattson was watching anxiously for Charlotte and the kids. B.J. smiled over at Jake as he stepped up to him.

"Damn, B.J. You know, I had a guy just hit on me back there, thanks to your little joke. That used to be one of my favorite bars. Now, how the hell am I ever going to be able to go back in there?"

"Oh, hell, lighten up, Jake. It was just a little joke. Boy, you have lost that old sense of humor ever since you went out with that reporter gal. What's the matter? She turn you down for a grand tour of your bedroom?"

Jake didn't answer.

"Well, I'll be damned. Finally ran into one that didn't fall under the ol' Mortimer spell, did we? You know, I—" Mattson stopped talking when he saw his son, Jason, come out of the tunnel. Behind him was Charlotte and their daughter, Angela. Forgetting Jake for the moment, B.J. rushed up to his son.

The boy stuck out his hand to his father. Jason felt he was getting too old now for that hugging business.

His father didn't see it that way. Grabbing the boy's hand, he pulled Jason to him and hugged him. "Great to see you, son."

"You, too, Dad," answered Jason, a little embarrassed.

Angela wasn't as inhibited. Running over, she wrapped her arms around her father's neck and squeezed tight. "Oh, Daddy, we've missed you. Are you all right? We saw you and Jake on television at least twenty times."

"I'm fine, darlin'. My, but you're sure growing fast, honey. Have to be beatin' those boys off with a stick pretty soon."

"Ooooh, Daddy!" she said, as she pulled away and ran over to give Jake a big hug.

Charlotte stood quietly to the side, not wanting to interfere with the reunion of the children with their father. Now, B.J. stood staring at her. It had been a long time for both of them. Eighteen months. She was still as beautiful as he remembered her. The *Playboy* centerfold body, the long, flowing blond hair, and the blue-green eyes that had enchanted him over nineteen years ago at Texas A&M. She reminded him of a Roman goddess. As he stepped toward her, she smiled into his blue eyes. The blond hair that he normally kept cut in a flattop seemed to shimmer under the airport lights. As he reached out to her, she stepped into his arms, and they kissed, a long, slow, lingering kiss. It had been a long time.

At Jason's and Angela's encouragement, Jake walked over to the couple who was still locked in an embrace, and whispered, "Okay, you two, you're both about three seconds from breaking the Florida obscenity laws."

The laughter from the couple broke their kiss. Charlotte turned to Jake. Kissing him on the cheek, she hugged him as she asked, "Jake, it's so good to see you again. How have you been?"

Mortimer returned the embrace and stepped back, smiling at the attractive woman. "Trying to stay out of trouble, Charlotte; but I've got to admit, working with your ol' man here, that's not an easy task, I assure you. Did he tell you he's going to be promoted to colonel day after tomorrow?"

Charlotte had a look of surprise on her face as she said, "Colonel!"

"Yeah, I was going to save it for a surprise, but I guess since my motor-mouth partner here has let the cat out of the bag, that's shot in the ass."

Jake shook his head sadly. "Sorry, B.J. You should have said something when we were in the bar instead of making everybody think I was gay."

Charlotte burst out laughing so loud that others in the area turned to stare at her. "Gay! My God, B.J., what have you been doing to this poor boy?"

"Just the normal crap. The general's going to pin the new rank on at the annual SOCOM family day picnic, day after tomorrow. That's another reason I wanted you to get here a couple of days early. You'll pin on one side while ol' Q-Tip pins on the other."

"But, honey, I would have still made it in plenty of time, even if I came in on tomorrow's flight as I had planned."

Mattson smiled as he tightened his grip around her waist and let his big hand roam down onto her firm buttocks. "Well, that wasn't the only reason I wanted you here as soon as you could make it. Eighteen months is a long time."

"You don't have to tell me that, B.J.," she answered, playfully moving her buttocks against his hand. "We'd better get home before we do get arrested."

Walking down the corridor to the front lobby, Jake asked Charlotte for her luggage checks. He and Jason would collect the bags while B.J., Charlotte, and Angela brought the car around. Digging around in her purse for the tickets, she found them and gave them to Jake. As he was about to leave, Charlotte asked, "Jake, be honest, now; with that stable of young women you always have around you, you never once suggested that my husband go out with a few of your girlfriends?"

Jake raised his hand. "I swear, Charlotte. The guy was like a hermit while you were gone. In the field or always at home watching TV. Couldn't get him to go anywhere."

"Well, I'm proud of you, darling."

"Oh, it wasn't that hard," said B.J., a mischievous grin etching its way across his face. "After all, what self-respecting officer wants to be seen in the company of a man suspected of being gay! If you doubt my word, just ask anyone in that bar over there."

Angela and Jason gave Jake a strange look. "Damn it, B.J., that isn't funny. Look at these kids! They just might believe that crap."

Charlotte and B.J. were still laughing as they took Angela and headed for the front door. Jake paused and looked hopelessly at Jason as he asked, "Anyone ever tell you what a real asshole your father is?"

Jason wrapped his arm around his uncle Jake and laughingly replied, "Yeah, Jake. My mom!"

CHAPTER 3

Ahmad Fisal slept nearly ten straight hours before Major Ruiz came to wake him as he had requested. The advance party, consisting of over half of the terrorist force, were preparing their equipment and would depart within the hour.

The sun hung only inches above the horizon. Darkness had already engulfed the base camp as Fisal and Ruiz approached the personnel packing their rucksacks with spare ammunition and C-4 plastic explosives. As the two leaders entered the lighted area, everyone stopped what they were doing and gathered around the sand table that had been constructed by Ruiz and his intelligence officers. The major areas of concern were highlighted in exact detail. Small, hand-carved wooden blocks identified the cities and outlying buildings around critical installations. Tinfoil from empty cigarette packs had been torn into small strips that were used to identify major river routes to be used by the boats in the operation. Larger pieces of wood had been hollowed out and filled with water to simulate the ocean running north and south along Florida's east coastline. Small piers and boat ramps had been painstakingly molded to detail and placed in their proper places along the coast.

31

Chipped pieces of red-orange coral identified the dangerous reefs and rock formations that would have to be avoided by the attack boats. The mock-up was an excellent piece of workmanship, constructed by experts.

Each team in the advance party had a specific function and a specific timetable in which to perform that function. They had been broken down into four seven-man groups, each team with a specific leader and a specified color designation.

In the early stages of the operation, Major Ruiz was concerned that the PLO members, who would be the last to arrive, would not have time to adequately study the objectives and rehearse their roles. Fisal had taken care of that problem. Photos of the mock-up were taken from all angles and delivered to the PLO squad leaders before their departure. Quizzes and rehearsals had been conducted all along the route of travel. If anything, the Palestinians were better prepared than those who had been in the swamps these last few weeks.

Fisal took the sharpened stick offered by Ruiz and stepped to the side of the sand table. Using the stick as a pointer, he placed the tip on a group of buildings located midway up the coast. The name tags that had been placed inside the objects on the table had been removed. Looking across the table at Mueller, Fisal said, "Blue Team!"

Mueller, attentive, but still possessing a look of overconfidence, stepped forward. "Depart base camp in approximately one hour. Move north until daylight, arriving at point Alpha, one mile south of Fort Myers. Conceal the team and allow them to rest until nightfall. At dusk, we will secure transportation and move to location Bravo, the town of Palmetto. Here we secure three boats from the Palmetto Marina and move into Tampa Bay. We will lie offshore until signaled by the Red Team under Mr. Imura and the Gold

Team under Captain Garcia that they are airborne and en route to the target area. I begin my attack run on the beach ten minutes after receiving their signal. We are to engage targets of opportunity with automatic weapons and grenades, providing confusion while a number of hostages are secured by the airborne teams. When the choppers have lifted off, I will swing my boats back to the entrance of the bay, where we will secure the boats to the pylons of the St. Petersburg Toll Bridge and set the timers on the explosives aboard the boats for twenty minutes. Eva will pick us up at point Charlie, located along Highway 41. Then we will return to our drop-off point on the outskirts of the swamp and make our way back to base." Mueller paused and smiled across the sand table at Fisal as he asked, "How did I do, professor?"

"Hopefully your success can equal your self-confidence, Herr Mueller. Have you established contingency plans, should you have to divert from our original plan?" asked Fisal.

"Of course," replied Mueller.

Looking around the table at the others, Fisal emphasized his remarks. "Keep in mind, gentlemen, your alterations to the original plan will be perfectly understandable; situations can change suddenly. You must be prepared to deal with those changes. Timing, however, is the one single constraint. Should any one faction not be in position at the appointed time, we will be courting disaster. Regardless of what else happens, you must adhere to the rigid timetable. Is that understood?"

The leaders around the table all nodded in agreement. Fisal turned to Imura. "Red Team!"

Imura leaned over the table and pointed to a group of small buildings located southwest of Tampa. "Red Team will depart within the hour in a northerly direction until we reach Highway 29. Here we commandeer transportation, continue up Highway 29, which intersects with Highway 27. Moving north, until we come to Highway 98, which leads to Fort Meade. Red Team will then establish a secure clandestine location and remain out of sight for the remainder of the day. At last light, we will move forward and take up positions at the edge of the chain link fence that surrounds the Army Reserve airfield. Beginning at 0530 hours, the team will cut this wire and enter the reserve area. This is a Reserve Air component of the Army. The bulk of their personnel do not report for duty until the weekend. As our attack will be made on a Friday, we expect to encounter no more than six to eight permanent duty personnel.

"Once all opposition has been silently eliminated, I will contact Gold Team that the area is secure and Captain Garcia will enter the installation with his pilots and begin the necessary checks on the five helicopters located on the east end of the field. Red Team will be responsible for security of the base until the helicopters are prepared to lift off at 0800 hours. On Captain Garcia's signal that he is ready to depart, we will then place our explosives at key locations within the installation, set our timers, and board the helicopters for departure to the primary target." Finished, Imura stepped back from the table and awaited any questions the Arab leader might have.

Fisal appeared pleased. "Very good, Commander Imura. Gold Team, you are next."

Captain Garcia came forward. "Gold Team will accompany Red Team to an area outside the installation. Once the area is secure and we have been notified, my team will enter the base and begin the primary checks on the helicopters to assure they are ready for lift-off. The helicopters are UH1H models, commonly referred to as Hueys by the Americans. Each ship is capable of transporting a crew of four and a

passenger load of six. Red Team and Gold Team will
constitute fourteen personnel. Mueller and Blue Team,
another seven. That gives us a total of twenty-one of our
people who will be aboard when the action is completed.
This leaves room for no more than twenty-nine hostages. I
would like to recommend that that number be limited to
twenty-five. That will assure us of an even distribution of
five hostages per helicopter."

Fisal nodded his approval, then eyed each of the other
leaders to see if they agreed. They did. "Continue please,
Captain Garcia."

"All pilots will lift off immediately once they have their
hostages aboard. They will not wait for the others. Once in
the air, they will fly to point Delta, which is an open field
three miles south of the town of Immokalee and adjacent to
the Big Cypress National Preserve. Upon hearing the
approaching helicopters, you and Major Ruiz will identify
the location for the pilots by marking the LZ with a yellow
smoke grenade. The hostages will be secured and the
choppers destroyed in place. We will all then move into the
swamp and back to base."

"Excellently done, Captain. That leaves only one final
detail. The actions of the Black Team. They will be led by
one of my most trusted lieutenants, Kamal Haddad." The
man called Haddad moved into the light. He was a tall, wiry
man with a beard and penetrating black eyes that seemed
lifeless in his swarthy face. Haddad's English left a lot to be
desired. Fisal, therefore, gave Black Team's portion of the
briefing.

"Haddad and seven of the Palestinian brothers will be
responsible for alerting the world to our intentions. So
there will be little doubt as to the seriousness of our threats,
the Black Team will provide a demonstration of our
destructive abilities. I have chosen an internationally known

location for just such a demonstration—one I am sure will gain us immediate world attention—Walt Disney World."

Ramon Garcia's eyes shot toward Ruiz. That was not the original plan. The terrorist target was to have been the power and light utilities in Miami. Ruiz saw the desperation in his captain's eyes. Most of those around the table were murmuring their approval of the target selection as Ruiz spoke up. "Mr. Fisal, sir, I would strongly recommend that we stay with the original target. Miami is a major city. To totally disrupt an entire American city's communications and power supply would bring that city to a dead stop. Would that not be enough of a demonstration of our powers?"

Mueller laughed loudly as he wrapped his arm around Eva and said, "Oh, look, my dear, the major is worried that someone might get hurt in this little game." Dropping his arm from her shoulder, Mueller leaned against the table. "What's the matter, Major? Have you no stomach for killing these American bastards?"

Ruiz was struggling to control himself. He had never wanted to kill anyone as badly as he wanted to kill this belligerent German bastard. Constraining himself, Ruiz replied calmly, "Killing is not a problem for me, Herr Mueller. I am certain you will have an opportunity to observe that fact before this is over. However, your knowledge of the Americans would appear to be as lacking as your knowledge of our Arab brothers. The Americans have grown timid over the years. Their taste for war and violence is not as prevalent as in past generations. But I warn you: an attack upon helpless children will bring down the wrath of not only the Americans, but also the entire world. I can see no possible way such an act could do anything but harm our cause. I would ask you that you reconsider the target, Commander Fisal."

All eyes were on the Arab leader as he pondered the Cuban's words. Ruiz was right. Disney World was a child's world of fun and fascination. Hundreds of children were sure to be killed. Haddad and his men would place over two hundred pounds of plastic explosives throughout the park. The death toll would be unimaginable. Yet, the news media would swarm over the bloody sight like vultures, fighting among themselves to be the first to bring live pictures of the blood and gore into the homes of millions of Americans. It was too bad they could not adjust the attack for later in the evening. Such a sight around suppertime would have more impact. To hell with the Americans. They had little concern when it came to Palestinian children dying. No, this would have the effect Fisal sought. It would serve as a strong warning of what would continue to happen if his demands were not met.

"I am sorry you feel as you do, Major Ruiz. However, I must think of our mission. After such an attack, the American people will force the men we want into these swamps. They will leave them little choice. The target will remain Disney World."

Ruiz sighed deeply and stepped back. A sick feeling gripped his stomach. He hadn't wanted this mission. He wanted it even less now.

"All right, then," said Fisal. "Everyone knows their responsibilities. Failure on the part of one will lead to the failure of the others. We must not fail. Most of the anti-intrusion devices and sensors have been put in place around the war zone. Major Ruiz, we will complete the installation of the radar units by tomorrow night. All will be ready by the time you return with the hostages. Then the game will begin. Are there any questions?"

No one had any. Ruiz had considered making one final plea for the target change, but realized it would be futile.

Fisal was looking forward to the bloodbath that was to come.

"Good luck, and may Allah be with us all," Fisal concluded. Then he added, "Miss Schmidt, could I speak with you privately for a moment? That is all, gentlemen."

Ramon Garcia waited until the group had scattered before approaching his commander. "Major, this is insane. You know that, don't you? No one is going to get out of here alive. It won't matter if we kill everyone in the elite American force. The death of those children will seal our fate."

"I know, Captain, but there is little we can do about it now. The decision has been made. All we can do is try to survive as long as possible. Now, go; you have a job to do."

Garcia's face saddened as he saluted and whispered softly, "Yes, sir," and turned to walk away. He had only gone a few steps when he stopped and looked back at Ruiz. "Major, the—the young girl and her friends who were captured by Fisal. Perhaps they could be released late tomorrow night? By the time they make their way out of the swamps, the game will have already begun, and everyone in the world will know where we are. There will be enough killing before this is over. They have suffered enough. Do you think that may be possible, Major?"

Ruiz felt a sense of pride as he stared into the young captain's eyes. It was good that men trained in the art of violence and war could still feel compassion. It was the mark of a true soldier. Ruiz smiled with admiration as he replied, "I will see to it myself, Captain. Now, go."

Garcia saluted a final time, then rushed off into the darkness to join his team. Ruiz filled a bucket with water and walked behind Fisal's hut to the tree where the young Americans had been tied. All four sat on the ground around the tree. A rope bound their hands together. "I have brought you some wat—" The bucket fell from the officer's hand as he stared at the golden-haired girl. Her face was an ashen gray. Her attractive eyes bulged out horribly, and her swollen, colorless tongue protruded from her lifeless lips.

Dropping to his knees, Ruiz stared at the rope that had cut into her throat. There was little blood. Moving around the tree on his hands and knees, he stared into the dead faces of the three boys. There were marks in the dirt beside the bodies where frantic hands had scratched and clawed for life—life that had been slowly, sadistically squeezed out of them. One of the ropes placed around the chests of the group had been raised to their necks, then a stick was intertwined in the rope. The stick had been slowly twisted, strangling the four teenagers to death.

Heartsick at the sight, Ruiz sat limply on the ground and stared at the once beautiful young girl. Fisal could have shot them. At least that would have been a quick death, not slow and agonizing as this surely had been. It was not until he looked up at the girl's body again that he suddenly realized that it had not been Fisal who had done this. The girl's blouse was open and her breasts exposed. Moving closer, Ruiz could see traces of red-orange lipstick and teeth marks around the small nipples. His hands tightened into fists as he clutched the moist ground in his hands and swore a silent vow to the dead girl. He swore he would kill the German bitch who had done this.

CHAPTER 4

Day 2—0730 hours
MacDill AFB, Tampa

"Hey, Mom, you and Dad going to spend the rest of the year in that bed? Come on down. Angela and I have already fixed breakfast for you guys, and we only caught the stove on fire twice!"

Charlotte pulled herself out of B.J.'s arms and sat up. "You don't think they really started a fire, do you?"

B.J. reached up and pulled her naked body back down on top of him. "I don't know, but right now I've got a little fire of my own going on."

Charlotte grinned as she stretched out on top of him and laid her head against his wide chest. His hands felt warm and strong as they rubbed the cheeks of her buttocks. "B.J.," she whispered, "why didn't you ever sit me down and explain how important your job here really was? I mean, I didn't realize how your job affected so many things in this screwed-up world. If I had known, maybe I would have been more understanding of why you didn't want to quit—why you felt it was so important."

"I just didn't want you to worry; that's all."

"Oh, but now I feel terrible. Here you are, constantly under pressure, and I add to it by acting like a spoiled little brat and running back home to Mama with your children. It's a wonder you don't hate me. I'm—I'm sorry, B.J. I really didn't know."

Mattson slapped her on one ass cheek; the stinging pop echoed around the room.

"Ow!" she cried.

"There! Now you've been punished for being a spoiled little brat, and that's the end of it, okay? Now, what are we going to do with this fire I've got going down there?" he said smilingly.

"I love you," she whispered. Kissing him hard on the mouth, she moved down his neck, then to his chest, her tongue darting out like a velvet snake across his nipples. B.J. shivered slightly, and she laughed. "My, my, Mr. Mattson, first a fire, now an earthquake. I wonder what will happen when I—"

"Mom—Dad! Come on, my masterpiece is getting cold." It was Angela this time. "Eat breakfast, then you can both go back to bed and—talk—the rest of the day if you want to. Please come down."

"We'll be right down, darling. Pour us some coffee, will you?" replied Charlotte.

"Okay, Mom."

Charlotte rolled off B.J. and went to the closet to get her robe. "Come on, honey, her grandmother taught her how to prepare the perfect breakfast. She wants to impress you. She does a pretty good job of it, too."

B.J. reluctantly swung his feet off the bed and put on his robe. Looking at himself in the mirror, he began to laugh. Charlotte peeked around the corner of the bathroom door to see what was so funny. "Oh, my God!" she shrieked as she began to laugh. B.J.'s fire down below had not subsided, and his robe stuck out like a circus tent on its side.

"Now, see what you went and did. How are we going to—"

Charlotte was grinning as she peeked around the door again and whispered, "Come on in here and let the fireman take care of that for you."

"All right!" said B.J. excitedly as he opened his robe and stepped into the bathroom.

A sudden splash of ice-cold water hit him in the pelvis area, and he howled, "Jesus!"

Laughing, Charlotte raced by the door, giving him a peck on the cheek. As she went by, she said, "Sorry about the water damage—but the fire's out! See you downstairs, darling."

She was out the door and on her way to the kitchen before he could answer. Pulling a towel from the rack, B.J. Mattson dried himself off as he muttered, "Looks like Jake was right. Everything is going to work out just fine." Tossing the towel on the hamper, he grabbed another robe, tied it around his waist, and went whistling down the hall to join his family for breakfast.

Charlotte hadn't exaggerated, Angela's cooking was exceptional. The table conversation covered everything from the horses on Grandma's ranch to the sudden hero status of SOCOM. The kids had never been happier, and it showed. There was a knock at the door. Charlotte answered it. It was Nancy Smith. Tommy and Nancy Smith had been longtime friends of the Mattsons. Tommy was the senior crew chief of SOCOM's Special Operations Wing and had been involved in a few of B.J.'s operations. Seeing the breakfast dishes, the attractive blond said, "Oh, I'm sorry, Charlotte, we didn't mean to interrupt your breakfast."

Charlotte pulled her on into the kitchen. "Oh, nonsense. We were through, anyway."

Jason and Angela both spoke at the same time. "Nancy, are Amber and Troy with you?"

"They sure are, and they're just as anxious to see the two of you." Waving out to the car, Nancy motioned for her kids to come in. The Smith children were the same ages as the Mattsons. The two sets of children were practically inseparable. Charlotte's leaving had been almost as hard for them as it had for B.J.

The kids disappeared off to their bedrooms as the grown-ups poured more coffee and talked for a while. B.J. excused himself and went upstairs to dress. By the time he had come back downstairs, the kids had taken off in Nancy's car to head for the beach. Charlotte was catching up on all the latest gossip, and B.J. was going to work. Things in the Mattson household had finally returned to normal. Kissing Charlotte on the cheek, B.J. left for SOCOM headquarters.

Master Sergeant Tommy Smith was standing with Jake and General Johnson at the reception desk when Mattson entered the headquarters. "Yo!" said Smith. "Here comes the soon to be full-bird colonel, now."

"Hero—extraordinaire," chanted Jake.

"Oh, give it a break, will you, guys? Morning, General."

"Morning, B.J. How's our local TV celebrity doing this morning?" asked J. J. Johnson with a grin.

"Oh, not you, too, sir," sighed Mattson.

Johnson laughed. Placing his hand on Mattson's shoulder, he said, "Come on into my office. I'll offer you a cup of coffee."

Jake and Tommy told B.J. they would see him later and

left. The general's secretary brought in the coffee and closed the door behind her as she departed.

"So, tell me, B.J., how are things on the home front?" inquired Johnson.

Mattson sat back in the large, overstuffed leather chair in front of the general's desk and took a sip of his coffee before he answered. "We're doing fine, sir. Charlotte and I had a long talk. We've worked out the problems and are starting from scratch again. Things couldn't be better."

The general smiled. He was happy that his top officer had managed to get his marriage and family back on track. Johnson glanced at the picture on the corner of his desk. It was the last picture ever taken of the general and his son. J. J. Johnson knew full well how personal problems could affect an officer's performance. His son's helicopter had been shot down by friendly fire during the Grenada invasion. It was a loss that had nearly ruined his career. Now, he looked upon Mattson not only as his top trouble-shooter for SOCOM, but almost as another son. The two men talked for a while about the last mission and the upcoming picnic. Johnson said that he was looking forward to seeing Charlotte again. Mattson inquired about Helen Cantrell, a lady the general had met in Washington who he had become very fond of over the past few months. For a man of sixty, the general was still ruggedly handsome and could turn the heads of more than a few women. Ms. Cantrell was flying down from Washington for the SOCOM affair.

Finishing his coffee, B.J. set the cup aside and leaned forward in his chair. His face took on a serious look, as he asked, "General, what about General Sweet? Are we finally rid of him? His actions on that last operation are

surely enough for you to ask that he be replaced in this
command."

Placing his fingertips together and bringing them up to
his chin, Johnson leaned back in his chair. He rocked
back and forth in silence for a moment. His steel-gray
eyes peered at Mattson over the top of his fingers.
Mattson had every right to want Sweet dumped. The man
had been nothing but a thorn in the side of SOCOM ever
since his arrival. Sweet was a conventional officer who had
little love for unconventional tactics and even less for
the men who ran such operations. Unfortunately, his
assignment to the unit had been one of the preconditions to
the funding of the Special Operations Command. Since
his arrival, he had tried in every way possible to manip-
ulate the unit into compromising situations that could
prove nationally embarrassing and raise questions about the
effectiveness of the command. Assisting him in this goal
were a number of high-ranking officials from the other
military branches, as well as a few highly placed congress-
men and senators. So far, Sweet had done little more than
embarrass himself and those who had placed him in the
command. A good example of that was the present closed
congressional hearings going on in Washington. However,
a man with friends in high places was seldom made to pay
the price for his mistakes. Sweet was just such a man. B.J.'s
resentment was understandable. Sweet's interference had
almost cost Jake and him their lives on more than one
occasion. Johnson doubted this last attempted interference
with a mission would result in a parting of the ways between
Sweet and SOCOM. Looking Mattson straight in the eyes,
Johnson said, "Son, I wish I could say he was out of here,
but I'm afraid that's not the case. Sweet somehow managed
to shift the blame to the Navy. I'm afraid he's walking away
clean."

"God damn it!" moaned Mattson as he slapped the arms of the chair.

"I know it's frustrating, B.J.—but, hey—tomorrow's supposed to be a celebration. Let's not give Sweet the satisfaction of ruining that for us, okay? We'll worry about him next week." Standing, Johnson walked around his desk. Mattson stood as the general came over and wrapped his arm around his shoulder. "B.J., you and Jake have done more than your share to bring respectability and honor to this unit. Thanks to you boys, tomorrow will be a day that marks our success. A lot of people didn't think we'd still be around this long, but we showed them we're here to stay, and they had better get used to it. I could not talk that way if it wasn't for you, son. Thank you."

Mattson could feel the bond that joined the two men tighten. It was more the bond of a father and son than a commander and an officer. "Thank you, sir."

The general's secretary tapped on the door and entered. "Sorry, sir, but you have two calls. One is the Tampa Bay Chamber of Commerce. It's about the awards dinner they are holding in your honor next week. They need to discuss a few details with you. The other one is Major Howerton, of the Florida Civil Air Patrol. There are some kids missing out in the Everglades. They want to know if SOCOM might be able to provide assistance this weekend, should a search become necessary."

"Fine, Sharon. Put Major Howerton through first. As long as it's for the weekend and not tomorrow, we'll give them a hand. B.J., I'm glad everything is working out for you. I'll see you later." Slapping the major on the back, Johnson went back to his desk. As Mattson was leaving, he heard the general say, "Major Howerton, I understand we may have some lost kids on our hands—"

Mattson was heading for his office when he saw Major Erin Hatch, the G-2 intelligence officer, going downstairs to the communications section. With little else to do, B.J. figured this would be a good time to catch up on the latest intelligence reports from some of the trouble spots in the world. Hatch saw Mattson enter the security area and waved a greeting. B.J. joined him at the situation board, a giant map of the world that covered the entire east wall of the room. Dozens of colored pins dotted the globe. Each represented either a full-scale war, guerrilla activities, or potential hot spots. As long as those pins were in that map, the people of SOCOM would have their jobs.

"What's up, Erin?" asked B.J.

"Not much. The boys in El Salvador took a few mortar rounds last night—nothing serious. No casualties. All in all, a pretty quiet night around the old globe. How's Charlotte and the kids?" he asked.

"Doing fine, thanks." Mattson let his eyes roam over the areas of the Middle East, then down to Cuba. "No problems out of our boy Fidel?"

Hatch laughed as he replied, "Nope, I think you guys hurt his feelings last time out." Hatch paused a moment and stared at the off-color pin he had placed next to Havana a few days ago. It served as a reminder. "Only thing we've had about Cuba came from the Israeli intelligence. Seems there have been a number of Palestinians going in and out of the country to confer with Fidel. Seems they're not happy with Fidel's explanation of what happened to their poison gas."

"Good," said B.J. "Anybody important missing from the board?"

Hatch laid his clipboard aside and looked at the map as he

answered. "Only our number-one terrorist, Ahmad Fisal. The Israelis lost him somewhere around Cyprus. He's reported to be in Cuba right now. The Massod is sending a few operatives in tonight to confirm that."

Mattson slapped Hatch on the back. "Well, looks like you got it under control, ol' buddy. You and the missus coming to the picnic tomorrow?"

"Wouldn't miss it, B.J. Not every day I get to see a major jump a rank straight to full-bird colonel. Congratulations."

"Thanks. We'll see you tomorrow," said B.J. Leaving the operations center, he walked back to his office. Jake and Smith were waiting for him. "Hey, what's going on, guys?" asked Mattson as he entered.

"Don't bother to sit down, partner. The general's declared the remainder of the day a training holiday."

"Yeah," said Tommy Smith. "What do you say we go by and pick up some beers, a few steaks, and do the ol' backyard barbecue trick?"

"Sounds good to me," said Mattson. "Jake, why don't you flip through that dictionary you call a little black book and bring a lady friend along."

"Great idea, B.J. I've got just the lady in mind. See you later."

Smith and Mattson strolled to their cars. "Think we should ask the ol' man?" suggested Smith.

"No, he's got to be at the airport to pick up Helen Cantrell this afternoon. I imagine he'll have other plans."

The two agreed to meet at the Mattson home later. Pulling out of the parking lot, B.J. turned on the radio as he drove away. "Authorities are still investigating the disappearance of four teenagers from the Fort Myers area. The party was last seen in the vicinity of the Bonita Springs area where they reportedly rented an airboat and were planning to explore the Big Cypress swamp. A search is expected to begin this weekend. In other news, officials at Disney World report attendance at Florida's number-one attraction will set a new record by the weekend."

CHAPTER 5

Day 3—0430 hours

Following Fisal's briefing of the night before, Mueller and the Blue Team departed the base camp. They made good time through the swamps and across the Caloosahatchee River, arriving north of Cape Coral one hour before sunrise. Mueller found a huge drainage pipe with a shallow spillway located only a few hundred yards west of Highway 41. The pipe provided the perfect concealment area for the men to spend the day resting from their rugged trip out of the Big Cypress Swamp. After nightfall, they moved once again, this time paralleling the highway until they came to the small town of Punta Gorda located at the edge of Charlotte Harbor.

It was here that Mueller planned to acquire the necessary transportation that would carry them the final fifty miles to the Palmetto Marina. Arriving at Punta Gorda a little after midnight, the German leader ordered his men to get some sleep. He would wake them when it was time to make the next move.

Day 4—0500 hours

As he sat staring out over the clear horizon, he watched in silence as a thin line of gray appeared between that horizon and the curtain of darkness. Slowly, reluctantly, the night gave way to the approaching dawn. It was time. Waking his men, he signaled for them to move toward the highway. Scrambling up the graveled incline that flanked the main road, the Blue Team took up prone positions near the edge of the asphalt.

Mueller paused at the rear of the team. Kneeling, he reached into the small knapsack that he carried and removed a silencer and his Beretta. Locking the long sound suppressor into place on the 9mm pistol, he moved up the line. During the long wait, Mueller observed that only a few vehicles traveled this highway during the early-morning hours. They could not afford to be selective in their mode of transportation. The next thing coming down this road was going to have to be it.

From somewhere along the line a voice spoke anxiously, "Herr Mueller, lights—someone is coming!"

Mueller moved out onto the highway. The vehicle was still a good half mile away. Pulling a small plastic bag from his shirt pocket, he directed one of the men to come forward and lie down on the side of the road. Tearing the plastic open, he held the bag over the man's face and squeezed the mixture of Karo syrup and red food coloring, letting it drain over the left side of the man's face and head, giving him the appearance of having a massive head injury. Tossing the bag off the road, Mueller stood and said, "Remain perfectly still. Do not move until I tell you to."

Looking back at the others, he motioned for them to stay down. The heads of the Blue Team disappeared as they inched their way back down the slope a few feet. Placing the silenced pistol in the small of his back, he pushed it down in his belt, stepped out into the oncoming lane of traffic, and waited.

Mueller could feel the adrenaline begin to flow as the lights of the vehicle slowly emerged from a small dip in the road less than a hundred yards away. The image of the vehicle was clearer now. "Perfect," whispered the German. It was a mobile recreational vehicle.

The lights were fifty yards away now. The beams of light swept over him as he began waving his arms over his head and pointing to the man on the side of the road. The vehicle slowed down. At first, he wasn't sure if it was going to stop. The driver swung over into the far lane as if he were going to go around him. Mueller began waving frantically; at the same time, he moved farther and farther over into the next lane. The RV slowed down even more and finally stopped.

Displaying a look of concern and panic in his face, Mueller rushed around to the driver's side of the vehicle. There was a Tennessee inspection sticker located in the lower left corner of the windshield. Perfect again—no one would miss them.

A man in his late sixties rolled down his window. His gray-haired wife sat on the passenger's side, her hand clasping her mouth as she stared in horror at the bloody sight on the side of the road. Another elderly couple came from the rear of the RV and peered out at Mueller from behind the seats.

"What happened here, young fellow?" asked the driver.

Providing just enough stress in his voice to emphasize near panic, Mueller blurted out, "My—my friend and I were walking along the highway when a car—a car swerved off the road straight at us. I jumped out of the way—but—but my friend was hit. We need help. Will you help me, please? I have to get him to a hospital."

"Oh, how terrible!" said the man's wife. "Of course we'll help you. George, you and Charles help the young man get his friend inside."

The two elderly men glanced at one another for a moment, then back at Mueller. Whether it was experience born of age or merely an unexplainable feeling, both men were hesitant. There was just something wrong with all of this. They became suspicious. Mueller, sensing that suspicion, played on the sympathy of the two elderly woman. "Please, every minute could be the last for my friend. In the name of God, won't you please help us?" Mueller had even managed to squeeze out a phony tear, which now ran down his cheek. That was all the women needed to see.

"George! You and Charles get out there and help that boy, or Martha and I will."

"All right! All right, we'll do it. You two stay in here. Come on, Charles," said the driver as he turned off the motor.

Mueller thanked the women and moved back to the body of the man on the road. The old men reluctantly came out of the RV. Their eyes darted back and forth and up and down the road as they walked over to Mueller and knelt down to look at the body.

"Jesus, George, sure looks like a mess, don't he?" said Charles.

"Yeah, well, let's get him inside. I don't like us bein' out here in the middle of no place like this."

Both women were staring out the windshield as their husbands bent down to pick up the injured man. It happened so quickly that the women had no time to react or to shout a warning. The gun seemed to appear as if by magic and bucked once in the man's hand. A small portion of George's hair at the back of his head flew up as he pitched forward across the legs of the man on the ground. Charles, his hands still cradling the underarms of the supposedly injured man, stared in momentary disbelief at the body of his friend. Then he looked up at Mueller. There was no fear, only hardened reality, as Charles muttered, "We fucked up."

"Exactly," said the German coyly as he pulled the trigger and shot the old man between the eyes. The impact tossed his body over the edge of the highway and into the line of men of the slope. "Now!" yelled Mueller. "Everyone into the van. Let's go!"

The women were screaming and crying as they fumbled with the keys to the ignition, trying desperately to start the RV, but it was far too late for that. Three of the men raced across the highway and entered the vehicle. The women were pushed and shoved out onto the highway. Terrified, they watched as the man with the bloody face who they had stopped to help, now tossed George's body off the road and down the slope where it came to rest against that of his friend Charles.

One of the women began to beg and plead with Mueller to let them go. They could have the RV. Tie them up and leave them in the trees off the road; it would be hours before anyone would find them. "Please! Oh, God, please don't kill us."

The other one, the driver's wife, looked up and down the highway. There were no lights coming from either direction. She knew it was hopeless. Her fear suddenly disappeared. It was replaced by a calmness that caught Mueller and the others by surprise as she said, "I would like to be holding my husband's hand when you do what you feel you must do. Will you permit me to do that?"

Mueller was amazed at the woman's courage. Her friend became hysterical. "No! No! You can't do this!" she screamed at the top of her voice. Mueller shot her in the

face. Blood splattered the side of the RV. As the body
bounced off the side of the vehicle and slid to the ground,
Mueller turned and offered his arm to the brave woman. No
words were exchanged, only silent glances. Placing her
hand on the German's arm, she walked slowly across the
highway and down the slope with him. The dead woman
was hoisted onto the shoulder of one of the men who
followed them. Silently, he held the body and watched as
the other woman knelt beside her dead husband. Bringing
the lifeless hand up, she kissed it, then lowered it to her lap;
she tilted her head forward.

There was no sound, only the sudden uplifting motion of
Mueller's hand as the shot was fired, and the woman fell
forward across her husband's chest. Mueller paused a
moment, staring down at her body. It was a perverted type
of honor, yet one of respect. Signaling for the other body to
be brought down the slope, he called for two more men to
help conceal his deadly deed. Satisfied that the bodies could
not be seen from the highway, he and the others returned to
the RV. One of the men had just finished wiping the blood
off the door, while another had spread dirt over the blood
spots on the highway.

Loading the team aboard the RV, Mueller slid in behind
the wheel and started the motor. Glancing at his watch, he
seemed surprised. The entire affair had taken less than ten
minutes. Placing the RV into gear, he pulled it back onto the
highway. They would be in Palmetto by 6:00 A.M. Relaxing
in the cushioned seat, he noticed a cassette player just below
the radio. Leaning forward, he pushed in the tape that had
been ejected when the travelers had stopped. The Blue
Team passed a road sign that read "Palmetto 48 Miles," as
the sounds of "Amazing Grace" carried across the deserted
landscape.

0530 hours
Army Air Reserve Installation
Fort Meade

Captain Garcia lowered his night vision glasses. Turning to Imura, he whispered, "Something is wrong. We have conducted reconnaissance on this installation for two months and at no time have there been this many personnel here on a Friday, especially at this hour of the morning. Something is not right. Have you maintained a count on the number of arrivals?" he asked.

Imura focused his glasses on the incoming vehicle that had just stopped at the main gate. He counted three more men in the car. Following the progress of the vehicle across the compound, he replied, "Counting the three who have just arrived, I place the number at thirty-six, and there are two more sets of lights approaching the gate from the highway."

"Damn," murmured Garcia. "What the hell is going on?"

Imura swung his glasses in the direction of the five helicopters sitting along the flight line at the end of the field. Fuel tankers were making their way across the runway and heading for the choppers. Crew chiefs were busy performing required preflight checks.

"Well, my Cuban friend, whatever the reason for this activity, we are going to have to make a decision as to our actions. Otherwise, we will have no helicopters. They are preparing them for lift-off right now."

Garcia raised his glasses once more and watched the crew chiefs swarming over the helicopters like small groups of busy ants. Imura was right. If the Americans maintained their normal preparation schedule, those helicopters would be airborne within two hours. The helicopters were the key to the operation. Without them, the chances of securing a reasonable number of SOCOM hostages and getting them back to the terrorist base where slim to none. Without the advantage of hostages, Mueller's beach attack and the Disney World massacre would be considered no more than simple terrorist actions which were sure to bring the wrath of the American military establishment down on the heads of Ahmad Fisal, Major Ruiz, and the others at the base camp.

Imura studied the worried face of his companion. He knew full well the implications of the decision facing the young Cuban officer. Already, they were outnumbered three to one. Taking out a few overnight staff duty people was one thing, but over forty? And it all had to be done in perfect silence, a task that seemed impossible. Imura had noticed a number of personnel rifles adorning the rear windows of many of the pickup trucks that had entered the installation. Then, there was the matter of the unit arms room. Already he had observed a few of the men exiting the operations room carrying pistols in shoulder holsters strapped across their chests. Garcia faced two very large problems, and he was fully aware of what those problems were. They were outnumbered three to one, and any attempt to overrun this installation was going to be anything but a silent affair. His losses would be heavy.

"It is regrettable that we do not have direct communications with the other elements. We could abort the operation and make another attempt next week," said Imura. Garcia nodded silently in agreement, but there was no communications link between the teams and the base site. The junglelike terrain, the dampness surrounding the swamp base, and the distances involved had made radio communications impossible without the establishment of a relay site somewhere between the Big Cypress Swamp and the elements involved. Such a relay site would have required an antenna system that would have to extend a minimum of thirty-four feet into the air. The sudden appearance of such a piece of equipment would have drawn the immediate attention of the Florida game wardens. The idea had been abandoned. Ironically, Garcia himself had been the one most strongly opposed to the relay site plan. It was an objection that now lingered painfully in the back of his mind.

Takeo Ohira, Imura's lieutenant, moved silently along the line until he found the two leaders. The stocky Korean knelt down next to Imura and whispered, "I took it upon myself to move closer to the wire in an attempt to discover why there is so much activity here this morning. It is the young ones—the young people that Fisal brought back to our camp. They are going to mount a search for them this morning. This unit has been asked to conduct an air search for the missing children."

Imura and Garcia exchanged knowing glances. Of course, the missing teenagers. Fisal had misjudged the speed and ability of the Americans to organize a search on such short notice.

Imura shook his head sadly and said, "I am afraid we have made a long trip for nothing, my friend. Without the helicopters, the game is over before it begins. Shall I order the men to pull back?"

Garcia looked at his watch. It was now 0615 hours. If everything else was still on track, Mueller would be nearing Palmetto Marina. Kamal Haddad and the Palestinians would already be in Orlando, preparing their explosives for the amusement park. The SOCOM event was not officially scheduled to begin until 0900 hours. Looking up at Imura, the young officer said, "Mr. Imura, I believe we should remain at least one more hour. There is always the chance that the situation could change in our favor, and as long as the helicopters are still on the ground, we have a chance."

A slight grin crossed the Japanese man's lips. "Of course, Captain. It would appear that you have had the same thought as I."

"What thought is that, sir?"

"That Ahmad Fisal is anything but a foolish man. I find it difficult to believe that a man who has survived as long as he has could not have foreseen the possibility of us encountering the very situation we now face. Perhaps I am wrong. Perhaps I give the man more credit than he is due. Either way, one more hour spent here is not time wasted to prove my profound evaluation right or wrong. Do you agree?"

"Precisely, Mr. Imura," replied Garcia. Pointing his finger to the south, the Cuban grinned. "And should we find our theories to be a matter of pure bullshit, Cuba is only ninety miles that way."

0600 hours
Fort Lauderdale Police Department

Eva Schmidt walked calmly down the steps of the police station to her rental van that was parked across the street. Humming to herself, she slid in behind the wheel, flipped on the radio, and drove away. Inside the station, the desk sergeant was placing a call to his captain.

"Yes, sir—that's right, sir. A lady just turned in the girl's purse. Says a girl and three boys spent the night drinking and raising hell in the sand a few hundred yards down from her beach house. She got up this mornin', the kids were gone, but she found the purse and came by to turn it in." There was a pause on the line; then, "Yes, sir, it's the girl who was reported missing, sir. Got her driver's license, a library card, and some credit cards with her name on 'em. Hell, she's probably afraid to go home after stayin' out all night. We done called the parents. They're a little hot under the collar, but relieved." Another pause; then, "Yes, sir, I'll get right on it. Good-bye, sir."

Hanging up the phone, the sergeant flipped through some papers on his cluttered desk until he found the number he was looking for. Picking up the phone again, he hit the buttons and waited. It rang twice.

"Major Howerton, this is Sergeant Baker of the Fort Lauderdale Police Department. The search has been called off. We think we know where the kids are. You can send your boys home."

0715 hours
Fort Meade

Garcia and Imura watched intently as one by one, the rotor blades of each chopper were secured in place with tie-downs. The crewmen removed their gear, walked back to the parking lot, tossed the kit bags into their cars, and left. Neither man was sure what had happened to bring on this sudden stand down, but they were not about to question their good fortune. Only four cars remained in the lot. These belonged to the men who performed the routine staff duties of the small base. All four were now inside the operations building having coffee and discussing the morning's events. As far as they knew, this was going to be nothing more than the usual boring day with a few extra hours thrown in.

Lowering his head, Garcia put his binoculars away and moved back from the small rise where he had just spent a very anxious hour. Signaling to the men on his left, he motioned for them to move forward and secure the flight line. Turning to Imura, he said, "Take the men on the right, circle around, and come in from the west. I will take the remainder straight in from here."

Imura nodded, then moved off to the right. Pulling his pistol from the holster hanging from his web gear, Garcia checked to be sure there was a bullet in the chamber. Removing a long, black silencer from the cargo pocket of his fatigues, he locked the heavy extension into place and gave it a twist. A strange sense of excitement began to course through his body as he stared at the quiet weapon of death. This wasn't Angola or Central America; this was the United States. Once he had pulled the trigger, the game would begin in earnest. There would be no turning back, nor would there be any escape. Win or lose, he knew they were all going to die. Allowing himself a moment to recall the faces of his mother and family in Havana, he whispered a silent prayer. Flipping the safety latch off the pistol, he wiped at the sweat that had formed along his upper lip. It was time to go.

Garcia waved his men forward. Low-crawling silently through the knee-high saw grass, they covered the distance to the chain link fence in a matter of minutes. One of the men moved to the wire and began cutting his way through the fence with a set of heavy-gauge wire cutters. The task accomplished, the man pulled the wire back. Garcia and the others scurried through the hole, raced across the compound, and hid themselves behind a pile of crates directly behind the operations building.

The Cuban tensed as he caught a glimpse of sudden movement out of the corner of his eye. It was Imura. They were through the wire on the right. They rushed the short distance across the open area. Flanking a side door to the operations room, they pressed themselves against the west wall. Imura signaled that he was ready.

Garcia acknowledged. Taking three of his men with him,

Garcia made a break for the rear of the building. Peering around the corner, he saw the main door was propped open. He could hear the Americans talking. Looking back to the security men he had left at the crates, he pointed to his watch, then raised two fingers. The security leader nodded that he understood, then relayed the signal to Imura. Watching the sweep second hand on his watch move toward the one minute mark, Garcia held a hand out flat. Imura's fingertips were poised on the digital timer of his Casio. His eyes were fixed on the relay man. As the second hand came up on twelve, Garcia's hand clenched into a fist. They would go in sixty seconds. Imura hit the timer as one of his men knelt near the door and began to slowly, quietly, turn the doorknob.

Edging his way along the wall, Garcia ignored the sweat that formed along his brow. His heart was pounding and his mouth had gone dry as he watched the second hand rush around the dial and head for the number twelve. He was less than three feet from the doorway when the moment came. He leaped into the doorway; the startled Americans looked up from the table, their coffee cups still in their hands. At the same instant there was a crash as Imura kicked open the side door and leveled his pistol at the two men closest to him.

"What the fuck—" The words were lost amid the noise of crashing chairs, screams, and moans of dying men as round after round of 9mm lead tore holes through their bodies. The Berettas held fifteen rounds. Garcia and Imura continued to fire until the slides of their weapons locked back in place, indicating that the pistols were empty. Shattered coffee cups, splintered wood, and pools of blood littered the floor. There was a moment of silence as the two assassins stared down at the mayhem they had rained upon their helpless victims. The smell of cordite was heavy, as a gray-white mist of gunsmoke drifted about the room. The pregame activities had begun.

Releasing the magazine from his pistol, Garcia slapped a fresh one into place and let the slide go forward. At the same time, he yelled to Imura, "Place four men at the main gate. Give them your pistol. They are to eliminate anyone who attempts to enter this installation before lift-off. Send the rest to the flight line. Preflight checks and fueling will not be necessary. Thanks to our friends here, we are now ahead of schedule." Garcia checked the time. It was 0735. They had calculated that the flight time from the base to Gadsden Point, the site of the SOCOM celebration, would take forty minutes. They had to be on station no later than 0900 hours to coordinate their attack with that of Mueller's beach assault. They had forty minutes to wait before lift-off. Garcia did not care to remain at the installation any longer than necessary, but they had little choice. The fuel load of the UH1H helicopters provided only enough air time for a straight shot to Gadsden Point, the pickup of the hostages, and a return to the landing zone at point Delta. Tossing his pistol to Imura, he said, "Here, give them this one, too. We cannot afford to draw attention to ourselves with the sounds of gunfire. Hopefully, no one will return here this morning, but we can't take that chance. Tell your men we will have a wait of forty minutes. They are not to leave their posts at the gate until the first four choppers are airborne. They will then lock the gate and board the final helicopter. Is that understood?"

"Yes, Captain, I will see to the gate security myself. Is there anything else?"

Garcia shook his head no. Imura left the room. Outside, men scrambled about as the Japanese leader shouted orders. Garcia picked up a coffee cup from a desk near the wall. Stepping over two of the dead men, he moved to the coffeepot and filled his cup. Blowing across the rim of the cup to cool it down, he noticed a large map of Florida hanging on a nearby wall. His eyes came to rest on Gadsden Point. He had to give it to Fisal; the man had balls. In a few hours the Americans were going to know just how big those balls were. Gadsden Point was a recreational area located on the southern tip of MacDill Air Force Base. It was not only the home for SOCOM headquarters, but also the Air Force's 56th Tactical Fighter Wing. Cuban intelligence estimated that at any given time there were no less than 100 F-16 Falcon fighters on the base.

The element of surprise would be the key. Garcia would take the helicopters in at treetop level to avoid the base radar. Once the attack began and the hostages were rounded up and placed aboard the choppers, what difference would one fighter or a hundred make? The awesome firepower of the Air Force fighters would be useless. They could hardly shoot down helicopters carrying captive Americans. Certainly, they would shadow the choppers to LZ Delta, but that would not matter. By then, Disney World would be in flames and Fisal's recorded message issuing the challenge to the leaders of SOCOM would be heard across the country. In that tape, the Arab leader would give the ground rules and location where the game was to be played. Copies of the cassette tape were scheduled for delivery to radio and television stations throughout the country at exactly 0900 hours this morning. The attack was, without a doubt, going to shake the very foundations of America, silencing those who boasted that the United States was invincible to terrorism.

Sipping on his coffee, Garcia walked out into the warm morning sunshine. He was staring across at the choppers when he heard a car approaching from the gate area. Imura was behind the wheel. The Asian pulled up alongside

Garcia, shut off the engine, and got out. Looking down through the windshield, Garcia saw the body of a young woman slumped against the passenger's door. A small trickle of blood trailed its way down her cheek from the small hole in the side of her head. "What happened?" asked Garcia.

Imura held up a white paper sack with the familiar golden arches on the side.

"She was bringing her husband his breakfast. Would you like to have it? It smells pretty good."

Garcia shook his head no. Imura shrugged his shoulders. Taking the sausage and egg biscuit from the bag, he took a large bite and began walking back toward the gate. His eyes still fixed on the lifeless body of the woman in the car, Garcia realized that it did not matter whether they won or lost the game. The aftereffects of their actions over the next few days would remain with the American people long after he was dead and buried. Their confidence would be shaken. They could never be sure when or where the next attack would come. After the final body count, they would never truly feel safe again. In the end, the terrorists would win the mind game. America would know the true meaning of terrorism and pay the price. Some already had.

0800 hours
Best Western Motel
Orlando

Kamal Haddad rinsed the razor and passed it to the next man. Wiping his face with a towel, he walked into the outer room and stared into the mirror, hardly recognizing the reflection without its familiar beard and mustache. Turning his attention to the other beardless men in the room, he watched as they prepared the final detonators and timers for their plastic explosives. Lifting the receiver from the phone near his hand, he called the room next to them. It rang twice.

"Yes," said the voice on the other end.

"Are you ready?" asked Haddad.

"Ten more minutes," came the reply.

"No more than that. We must leave here in exactly fifteen minutes."

"We will be ready."

Haddad replaced the receiver. Walking to the closet, he removed a brightly colored Hawaiian shirt from a hanger and slipped it on. Stepping in front of the mirror again, he evaluated his appearance as he buttoned his shirt. The deep, Middle Eastern tan would draw little attention here. If anything, he worried that the ridiculous looking shorts and colorful shirt would attract more attention. But he had been reassured by Fisal that the clothes they had purchased were typical of the American tourist. Moving to the drawn curtains, Haddad parted them slightly with his fingers and looked out across the motel courtyard. Fisal was right; they had all the necessary items: Bermuda shorts, eye-straining colorful shirts, tennis shoes, and sunglasses. Their attire guaranteed them the ability to move unnoticed among the crowds at the park.

Moving back to the closet, Haddad smiled to himself. In his twenty years as a terrorist, he was convinced this was going to be the most deadly, yet the easiest assignment he would ever have. The Americans did not bother with the elaborate precautions or complicated security systems that their European neighbors were forced to utilize. There was no need for it. Americans could come and go as they pleased. It was their right under their great Constitution. Haddad and his men were going to use that inalienable right to carry their explosives into the very center of Disney

World. Removing a light-blue knapsack from the top shelf, he opened it and removed the passes that had been purchased for today's activities at the park. The Americans made it so easy. Everyone carried one of these little backpacks for their valuables or whatever else they wanted to take through the park with them, and God forbid should anyone dare question what the sack contained or ask that they submit to a search of their private possessions. After all, they had their rights.

Watching his men place the charges in their knapsacks and zip them closed, Haddad was grateful to those Americans who screamed the loudest about the invasion of their privacy. However, after today, they might have to reevaluate the finer points of that right. The phone rang.

"Yes," said Haddad.

"We are ready."

"Good. Have the drivers bring the vans around."

Hanging up the phone, Haddad smiled at the men in the room who stood with their bags of death strapped across their shoulders. "Come, my brothers, it is time for our visit to the monument these Americans built in honor of a rodent."

0800 hours
Palmetto Marina

Mueller broke the latch off the cabinet that contained the keys for the boats moored in the marina. His eyes raced along the rows of numbers until he found the three sets of keys he was looking for. Pulling them from the hooks, he tossed them to one of the men at the rear door. "Get the men on board and start the engines, I will be there in a minute."

Catching the keys, the man headed down the long ramp leading to the boats.

Moving to the front door of the caretaker's building, Mueller moved the blinds aside and pulled the small cardboard clock from a nail. Setting the hands to 9:00 A.M., he placed it back in the window and fastened the blinds in place. Walking behind the counter, he bent down and checked the body of the old man on the floor. Two small bloodstains dotted the left pocket of the caretaker. Satisfied that the man was dead, Mueller went out the back door, locking it behind him. The only sound in the room was the sound of cardboard scraping against the plastic of the blinds as it swung back and forth from the nail. The caretaker was out, but he would not return at 9:00 A.M.

0815 hours
Fort Meade

Garcia sat on the edge of his seat and stared down at the men running from the gate. He watched them until they disappeared into the last helicopter. The final chopper slowly lifted and rose to join the others. Removing the headset from the hook above his head, Garcia keyed the radio. "Red One, this is Gold One. Are we ready? Over."

"Roger, Gold One. All personnel aboard. Over."

"Roger, Red One. Gold One, out."

The pilot looked back over his shoulder at Garcia. The Cuban raised a finger, circled it in the air three times and pointed to the west. The pilot banked left, dropped altitude to treetop level, and gunned the chopper forward. The other four helicopters came on line with the leader, flanking Garcia, two on the right, two on the left.

Below, people paused and stared up at the low-flying formation that rattled windows as it passed overhead. On a nearby golf course, two elderly men halted their game to watch the flyover. "Boy, them fellows are sure flyin' low this morning. Wonder where they're off to?" asked one of the men.

Shading his eyes, his partner watched the approaching birds. He answered, "Must be heading for that big SOCOM shindig they have planned over at MacDill today. CNN is going to be carrying part of the ceremony live beginning at nine o'clock." The man squinted his eyes as the UH1Hs passed directly over their heads. His friend had already returned to the game, positioning his putter behind the golf ball farthest from the hole. "Hey, Max—look at that! Never seen them do that before. They got machine guns mounted in the side doors."

CHAPTER 6

Over half of the command and their families were already
present for the day's activities. More were arriving all
the time. There was a joyous holiday atmosphere throughout the Gadsden Point Recreational Area. Volleyball nets
were being put in place, horseshoe pits stepped off, and
charcoal poured into the barbecue grills around the grandstand area. Most of the kids had already shed their clothes
in favor of beachwear and the warm waters of Tampa Bay.
The Mattson and Smith youngsters were among them.
General Johnson spotted B.J. and Charlotte near the grandstand. It wasn't that hard. General Johnson, Jake, and B.J.
were the only three members of the command who were
wearing fatigues. With the entire country watching, they
couldn't very well pin colonel's wings on a sports shirt. It
wouldn't bother them all that much, but the president
was planning to watch the ceremony on television at the
White House. The only other uniforms present belonged to
General Kelley, the MacDill base commander, and two of
his staff officers. This was supposed to be a unit party, not

71

an inspection. As soon as the ceremony was over, both men would change into something more suitable for the occasion.

The general waved for the couple to join him. Looking around, Johnson called to Helen Cantrell, the attractive widow he had met in Washington over a year ago. She had brought new meaning into his life. She made him feel young again, the first woman to affect him that way since his wife had died ten years ago. He loved her, and he knew she loved him. It was only a matter of time before he planned to ask her to marry him. If she thought this was a party, wait until their wedding; he would show her what a real SOCOM party was.

The mere sight of her long shapely body clad in tight white shorts and a straining halter top excited him as she strolled gracefully to his side. God, she looked good! No one would ever take her to be a woman of fifty-five. She didn't look a day over thirty. "Yes, Jonathan, what is it, dear?"

Wrapping his arm proudly around her small waist, he pointed to the Mattsons as they approached. "I want you to meet one of the heroes of our dynamic duo."

B.J. reached out and shook the general's hand. "Good morning, sir. Looks like a perfect day for this affair."

Johnson pumped B.J.'s hand a moment, then flashed a fatherly smile at Charlotte. "Glad to see you here, Mrs. Mattson. I'm sure you're as proud of this boy as we are."

Charlotte squeezed B.J.'s arm and replied, "Yes, General, very proud."

"B.J., Charlotte, may I introduce Ms. Helen Cantrell, my—my, uh—my companion."

B.J. couldn't help but grin. He had never known ol'

Q-Tip to be at a loss for words. Helen Cantrell was smiling as well. "Companion! My lord, Jonathan, that makes me sound like a perfect prude." Reaching out, she shook B.J.'s hand as she said, "What John was trying so delicately to say is that I am his girlfriend—his permanent lay, I believe is what they say these days."

The general turned a bright red and his mouth fell open. B.J. cracked up laughing at the sight. Charlotte laughed as well, then asked, "How long have you two been an item, Helen?"

"A little over a year now, Charlotte," she answered.

Johnson was still too stunned to talk. Charlotte reached over and patted the general on the shoulder. "Now, now, General Johnson, she couldn't help that. You Special Operations boys just have a way of bringing out the pure animal in a woman. Helen, would you care to go to the powder room with me? I'm sure the boys have a lot to do before the ceremony begins."

"Of course, Charlotte, I'd love to." Kissing Johnson on the cheek, she and Charlotte walked away.

"Quite a woman you have there, sir," said B.J.

"Yes, I never fully appreciated her until now. You know, I think your wife has something there—I mean, the pure animal theory and all. God, Helen would have never talked like that a year ago."

"Well, sir, let's just say the lady has a lot of class and a Special Op's attitude. I'd say she's going to fit right in around here."

Jake Mortimer rounded the corner of the platform. Beverly Mills was with him. "Yo, General, B.J., there you are. Been looking all over for you. Gentlemen, I'd like to introduce Ms. Beverly Mills, the most proficient and sexiest member of the CNN News staff. Beverly, this is my boss,

General Jonathan J. Johnson, and of course, my partner, Major—soon to be Colonel—B. J. Mattson."

The stunningly beautiful brunette with the blue-green eyes smiled at the two men as she said, "Gentlemen, it is a pleasure to meet you. I've seen you both on the nightly newscast. It is indeed an honor."

Johnson and Mattson were both humbled in the presence of the woman's beauty and her high praise. "Are you here for the party, or are you working, Ms. Mills?" asked Johnson.

"A little of both, sir. SOCOM is still big news across the country. Americans want to know more about the organization and the people who make it work. We plan to go live for the ceremony. We'll pull the plug after you and Mrs. Mattson pin the major's new rank on his collar." Pausing, she turned and pressed her well-rounded breasts hard against Jake's arm and continued, "Then, it's party time."

Now it was Jake's turn to blush. Before he could say anything, General Kelley called for the trio to join him at the grandstand. It was ten minutes to nine. Beverly gave Jake a quick kiss and left to join the television crew standing in front of the stage. Readying her microphone, she winked at Jake as he went up onto the stage. Helen and Charlotte had returned from the powder room. Charlotte joined B.J. on the stage. Helen sat with Tommy and Nancy Smith, who Charlotte had introduced Helen to on the way to the ladies' room. The crowd began to gather around the stage as General Kelley stepped behind the podium and laid out his prepared speech. He looked down at Beverly Mills and waited for the cue from the reporter that would signify they were on the air.

Charlotte could tell her husband was nervous. He was not

the type to enjoy being the center of so much attention. Slipping her hand into his, she squeezed it softly and smiled as she whispered, "It'll be over in a few minutes. Hang in there, Green Beret."

Mattson winked at her as he gripped her hand tightly. Beverly Mills held up three fingers, signaling they were three minutes from airtime. B.J. looked past her and out toward the beach. Some of the kids had already started playing volleyball. Others were laughing and splashing about in the water. Three sailboats were making their way out from Papys Point. Their colorful sails billowed in the wind. Beyond them, there were three large speedboats. Cigarette boats, they were called. Long and sleek, with twin inboard engines capable of turning speeds of up to eighty miles an hour. Huge geysers of water rose from the fantails of the speedboats as they swung in toward Gadsden Point. They must be moving awfully fast to throw water so high in the air.

Beverly Mills raised one finger. Suddenly, B.J. heard a familiar sound in the distance. It was coming from the southeast. Johnson and Jake had heard it, too. Helicopters— a lot of them.

"We're live in five, four, three, two, one, go," said one of the news crew.

"This is Beverly Mills, coming to you live from Gadsden Point Recreational Area, MacDill Air Force Base, in Tampa, Florida, where this morning, the Special Operations Command is holding its annual unit organization day ceremonies and honoring one of its heroes with a promotion to the rank of full colonel. We have as the guest speaker—"

B.J.'s eyes flashed back to the beach. The speedboats were less than 100 yards out and still had not decreased their speed. He could see the reporter talking into the microphone, but hadn't heard a word she was saying. Most of the kids had stopped playing in the water and were staring out at the oncoming boats. Mattson was about to yell for the kids to get out of the water when the five UH1H helicopters roared across the treetops and banked left directly above the stage. The downdraft from the propellers sent General Kelley's speech blowing in all directions. Dust and sand whirled up around the news crew and the audience. General Kelley was furious. He yelled at his staff officers and pointed angrily toward the choppers as they circled around again. They could do no more than shrug their shoulders. They had no idea who was flying them, or which unit they belonged to.

B.J. grabbed the general's arm and pointed to the boats. Jake was on his feet. He had seen it at the same instant. Orange-red flashes were coming from the boats that were gearing down less than twenty-five yards from the beach. The noise of the choppers had drowned out the sound, but Jake and B.J. knew a muzzle flash when they saw it. The people in those boats were firing at the beach. Any doubts suddenly disappeared as three of the kids on the beach grabbed at their chests and stomachs. The exiting bullets blew massive holes out their backs and rained blood onto the white sand. The other kids began to scream as they scrambled to get away from the beach. Small splashes of water jumped in the air around those who had not yet reached the beach. One by one they were hit, and they sank in puddles of blood.

Beverly Mills stared in shock at the slaughter that was going on before her eyes. She could not speak. The CNN crew swung their cameras toward the beach and televised the nightmare live across the nation. "My God, B.J., the kids!" yelled Charlotte as she leaped out of her chair and cleared the stage in one bound. Everyone on the stage did the same. People were screaming and running in all directions. The men were out of the boats now. The camera zoomed in on the tall blond man in battle fatigues who was shouting orders to his followers as they advanced toward the mass of terrified people near the stage. Helen Cantrell fell and was trampled before Johnson reached her and pulled her to her feet. "God, Jonathan, who are those people?"

"Terrorists!" he yelled, trying to be heard above the screaming and panic that surrounded them. "Helen, try to get the people to run for the parking lot. Hurry! It's their only chance." He screamed the same order to Jake and B.J., who tried, but found that it was hopeless. The panic was too great.

Nancy and Charlotte saw their kids coming at a dead run for the stage. A line of bullets tore up the sand only inches behind them. As they reached their parents, out of breath and frightened, the mothers hurried them toward the parking lot.

Tommy Smith had raced to his car. Opening the trunk, he pulled a .45 caliber Colt Commander automatic and a twelve gauge shotgun out from under a blanket. Shoving extra ammunition into his pockets, he raced back toward the beach. For the terrorists, it was a turkey shoot. Screaming, hysterical men and women attempted to shield their children from the swarm of lead that seemed to come from all directions, ripping, tearing, shredding flesh as round after round found its mark.

Jake pulled Beverly under the stage and out of the line of fire as a row of bullets danced their way through the sand, then hit the two men from her news crew. She screamed as the soundman's head exploded. His blood splattered one of her hands. The scream drew the attention of one of the gunmen. Dropping an empty magazine from his AK, he locked a fresh one into place. A sadistic grin crossed his face as he knelt down and pointed the weapon directly at Jake and the woman. Jake placed his hand over Beverly's face. He didn't want her to see it coming. The terrorist widened his grin as he duck walked a few feet closer to his victims. Jake's patience was at an end. "Do it, you son of a bitch!" screamed Jake as he closed his eyes and waited to die.

The smile dropped from the killer's face as he raised his rifle. There was a loud boom that came from somewhere above Jake's head. He opened his eyes in time to see the terrorist pitch backward. Half of his face was gone.

"What the—"

Tommy Smith leaped from the stage and hit and rolled in the sand only a few feet in front of Jake. Pulling the Colt automatic from his waistband, he held it out to the Navy man.

"Here ya go, Commander. I think it's time we started gettin' a little payback from these assholes!"

Smith didn't have to say it twice. Grabbing the gun, Jake reached over and pulled Beverly out from under the platform and to her feet. The very weight of the pistol in his hand restored his confidence. He was no longer a helpless victim.

Smith dashed to the side of the dead terrorist. He pried the rifle from the man's hands and was running back to the stage when General Johnson and Helen Cantrell suddenly rounded the corner. Two terrorists were chasing them. Smith's actions were more reflex than planned as he yelled, "General!" and tossed the AK to Johnson. "It's hot," he added, indicating that the rifle was loaded and the safety off.

The general pushed Helen to the ground with one hand while he grabbed the rifle out of the air with the other. Twisting, he dropped to one knee and fired, catching the lead terrorist with three rounds in the chest. The second terrorist never had a chance as both Smith and Jake caught him in a cross fire of twelve gauge double-odd buck and four .45 slugs from the automatic.

Jumping to his feet, Jake yelled for Helen and Beverly to make a run for the parking lot. They provided cover fire. Shaken and scared, the two women kicked off their shoes and made a wild dash for the lot. Scrambling to Johnson's side, Jake knelt down beside his commander and asked, "Are you all right, sir?"

Smith joined them, shoving more rounds into the shotgun as Johnson said, "Yes, I'm okay. That was close. God, it's a slaughter out there, Jake. Must be sixty, seventy people down out there. I don't see how it could get any worse. If the—"

Multiple sounds of machine gunfire from the sky brought an abrupt end to the statement as he and the others stared up into the clear blue sky. "Oh, sweet Jesus," cried Smith. "They're strafing the parking lot."

The sounds of screaming sirens were barely audible over the machine gunfire and the roar of the helicopters.

"About goddamn time," yelled Jake. "This whole fuckin' thing has been going out on national television for Christ's sake."

"Yeah, Jake," replied Tommy Smith, "but those boys ain't gonna be no match for five choppers with door-mounted M-60s."

The pilots of the Hueys must have overheard the veteran crew chief. No sooner had three Air Force security jeeps come to a stop at the wooden rail fence at the edge of the park, than two of the birds flanked all three vehicles.

Hovering at 300 feet, the door-gunners blew the jeeps and the occupants to pieces. The center vehicle exploded, engulfing the other two in a ball of flame.

"God damn it!" cried Johnson in frustration.

"Uh oh," exclaimed Smith, "those choppers are preparing to land."

"Good," said Jake as he loaded another magazine into the pistol.

Smith cast a sideways glance in the general's direction and shook his head. The commander of SOCOM was checking the number of rounds he had left in the AK.

"Uh—excuse me, General, sir—I, uh—know I'm only a lowly sergeant and all, but I think if you'll look around, you'll see we're the only good guys with guns—and damn little ammunition. Them boys got at least seventeen or eighteen bad guys and ten fuckin' machine guns on five choppers. Now, I ain't no tactician, but I'd say Custer had better odds than we got here."

Jake slapped the magazine back in his pistol as he said, "Shit, Tommy, we have to do something. We can't just sit here and watch this massacre."

Johnson laid the rifle across his knee. His eyes were searching the parking lot for some sign of Helen. There was no one moving in that direction. Only bodies littered the area now. Sergeant Smith was right, of course. They had no chance. His concern for Helen and the others had momentarily clouded his judgment. "Tommy's right, Jake. We can't do a damn thing with only three guns."

"Well, sir," said Smith with a sigh, "there is one thing—we can get the fuck out of here."

The choppers had landed. Terrorists leaped out the doors and raced for the parking lot to round up people who were hiding behind cars and in the trees beyond. Jake cast a stunned look in Smith's direction and said, "But, Tommy—your wife and kids are out there."

Pain registered in the leathery face of the rock-hard sergeant's eyes. "Yes, sir, they are. But I can't do 'em much good if I'm layin' deader than hell out there in that sand. If they're still alive, they know I'll be comin' for 'em. Dead, we got no chance at all of gettin' them back."

Johnson reluctantly nodded in agreement. Getting themselves killed wasn't going to help anybody. The shooting had died down to a few sporadic shots along the beach. Now was the time to get away. Low-crawling, they made their way beyond the rail fence and slipped into the trees. Pausing to catch their breath, they watched the terrorists loading men, women, and children onto the first three helicopters. Each man strained his eyes in hopes of catching a glimpse of a wife or girlfriend, but it was impossible. The terrorists had left the choppers running, it was a hot load procedure designed for quick in and quick out. The dust and sand being blown about by the rotors obscured any hope of positively identifying anyone from this distance.

"Wonder what their demands will be?" asked Smith.

"No telling, Tommy," said Jake. "The usual shit, I would imagine. A ton of money and the release of their terrorist brothers in Europe and Israel."

The roar of the speedboats drew the trio's attention back to the beach. At least there were no hostages being placed on the boats. The three Americans winced in helpless anguish as they watched two of the terrorists stroll casually down the beach a few yards and fire a burst of automatic weapons fire into the bodies of three kids who lay wounded in the sand. Laughing at their handiwork, they slung their rifles over their shoulders and returned to one of the boats. A tall, blond man gave the signal, and the three boats shifted into reverse and backed out into the bay, clear of the shallow water. A second signal, and the heavy engines roared, throwing water ten feet into the air as they swung left, speeding off for the St. Petersburg Toll Bridge at the opening of the bay.

There was the sound of more sirens screaming their way toward Gadsden Point. In the sky above, a flight of F-16 Falcon fighters banked and swooped down over the bodies littering the park. Johnson knew that their appearance was of little use. The terrorists already had hostages aboard the choppers. Right now, one of those pilots would be warning the MacDill control tower of that very fact. Any action by the fighters, and the hostages would die. Hell, Johnson didn't need to hear the conversation. He knew the scenario. He should; he had taught classes on terrorism at the war college. This kind of situation, after all, was what the Special Operations unit had been formed to prevent. Looking around at the bodies scattered on the sand, it was apparent that SOCOM and America had paid a terrible price for their myths of invincible power and overconfidence.

After the first three helicopters were loaded, they lifted off, heading back to the southeast. Watching them pass over their heads, Jake said, "I wonder what happened to B.J.?"

B.J. Mattson stood with his fingers interlocked and his hands resting on top of his head. He bit at his lower lip as he watched Charlotte, Angela, and Jason being pushed at gunpoint toward the fourth chopper. Every fiber of his being screamed to do something—anything—to stop this madness. However, such a move would be suicide. Two Asian girls in battle dress stood five yards across from him, their AKs leveled at his chest. One move and he had little doubt they would blow him in half. It wasn't just his life that would be lost. Nancy Smith and her two kids, along with three other women, had been grouped around Mattson. If he tried anything, they would all die.

A Cuban came over from the fourth chopper and pointed to Nancy and her two children, then toward the chopper. Troy Smith, a husky seventeen-year-old, curled his lip defiantly at the man, then spit on the Cuban's boot before saying, "Fuck you, asshole!"

The Cuban's hand shot out so fast that it was no more than a blur. The fist caught the teenager in the pit of the stomach and instantly doubled the boy over. He fell to the ground, gasping for air. His sister, Amber, screamed and covered her face as she began to cry. "You son of a bitch!" cried Nancy Smith as she knelt over her son and wrapped her arms around him to protect him from further blows. B.J. could tell by the look in the eyes of the Asian girls that they were getting nervous. Their fingers began to tighten on the triggers of the Russian assault rifles. Another Oriental—Mattson figured him to be Japanese—ran up to the Cuban who had now drawn his pistol with the full intention of shooting Troy Smith in the back of the head.

"What are you doing, you fool!" said the Japanese angrily. "We must hurry. Put that thing away and get these people on board and do it now! We have no time for this nonsense."

The pressures of the moment proved to be more than one of the women standing behind Mattson could bear. Dropping her hands and screaming, she turned and tried to run. B.J. reached out and grabbed Amber's arm, pulling her to the ground just as the Asian girls cut loose. They fired three short bursts on automatic, killing the fleeing woman and the other two who had been standing next to Mattson.

"Enough!" shouted Imura, stepping forward and waving for the women to stop firing. B.J. saw his chance. Swinging out with his left leg, he trapped Imura's foot, twisted the little man slightly, and kicked out with his right foot. The blow caught Imura behind the right knee and sent him falling backward onto Mattson's chest. B.J.'s left arm closed in a choke hold around Imura's neck while in the same instant his right hand pulled the Japanese terrorist's pistol from the holster at his side, placing the barrel of the weapon against Imura's head. Both girls and the Cuban took a step forward.

"Yeah, you come on, motherfuckers. One more step and I splatter this guy's brains all over Florida. Now, back off," yelled B.J.

Mattson wasn't exactly sure who the man he was holding was, but he had to be somebody important. The girls moved quickly back without the slightest hesitation. A look of concern was in their eyes.

"You, too, Poncho," said B.J., pressing the barrel even harder against Imura's temple. "You back off, or I swear I'll kill the son of a bitch."

The Cuban's eyes darted up suddenly. He was staring past Mattson. Someone was clapping his hands. Leaning his head back, B.J. stared up at a Cuban officer standing only a few feet away.

"Bravo, Major Mattson. A very impressive move," said Garcia with a smile. "However, we both know that you have no chance of achieving anything by this. Your heroics will only result in the needless death of this woman and her children." Walking around to the front of Mattson, he stopped and continued, "I said their death, not yours, Major. For you see, you are one of the main reasons we have come. Come, now, Major, release Mr. Imura and return his weapon. I know you do not desire the death of this poor woman and her children. You have my word, if you do as I have asked, no one else need die."

B.J. had always figured he would go out in a blaze of

glory when his time came, and this seemed the perfect opportunity, but not at the expense of his best friend's wife and kids. Slowly, he released the hold on the Japanese and let the gun fall from his hand.

"Ah, very good, Major Mattson. I knew I was dealing with an intelligent man," said Garcia, waving for the Smiths to be taken away.

Imura picked up his pistol, brushed the sand away, and replaced it in his holster. Bowing slightly at the waist and looking down at B.J., Imura said softly, "I salute you, Major. It would appear our reports as to your various abilities and courage have not been exaggerated. It is good that we shall be facing such a worthy opponent in the game."

B.J. sat up and brushed the sand from his hands as he asked, "What game? Who are you people and what do you want?"

Captain Garcia removed a cassette tape from his shirt pocket and passed it to Mattson. "The answers to all of your questions may be found on that tape, Major. I was to leave it with someone before we departed. It would seem that fate has intervened at a most opportune time to allow me to deliver this message to you personally."

Mattson stared blankly at the cassette, still not sure what this was all about. The flight of F-16s screamed past overhead. Garcia glanced skyward for a moment, then back to Mattson. "Now, if you will excuse us, Major, we have a long way to go and much that still remains to be done. We shall see you again in a few days. Adios, amigo."

Imura bowed again and joined Garcia. B.J. sat staring after the two men until they stepped into the choppers and lifted off. The fading sounds of the rotor blades were replaced by the high-pitched shriek of sirens as dozens of police cars and ambulances began arriving on the scene. Turning the cassette slowly between his fingertips, B.J.'s eyes wandered over to the bodies of the three dead women lying near him. He quickly turned away from the bloody sight. Rising to this knees, he leaned forward, resting his head on trembling hands as he whispered, "Oh, Charlotte, I'm so sorry I got you and the kids into this."

CHAPTER 7

A haunting silence hung over the conference room located in the basement of the Special Operations Command as the unit's key personnel awaited the arrival of Major Erin Hatch, the G-2 intelligence officer. General Johnson sat at the head of the table, staring at an enlarged map of the Florida Everglades hanging on the wall across the room. Others in attendance were B. J. Mattson, Jake Mortimer, Master Sergeant Tommy Smith, and Dan Hampton, regional chief of the FBI's Florida division. Across from him sat Richard Decord, the lieutenant governor of the state of Florida. The man was visibly shaken by the loss of life and destruction he had seen. The six men in the room sat in silence, each with his own thoughts. The shock of this morning's attack against SOCOM had certainly stunned the residents of Florida, as well as the nation. As bad as that attack had been, it was overshadowed by comparison to the staggering loss of life that had been inflicted on the unsuspecting masses at Disney World. At last count, the death toll stood at 235 killed and over 300 wounded. Most were children. Ninety-six people were reported missing and presumed dead following the explosion and collapse of over half of the St. Petersburg Toll Bridge. Four hours after the attacks, fires were still burning out of control. Walt Disney's dream was going up in smoke and nations around the world were watching it in living color on television in stunned disbelief.

Panic and rage gripped the political leaders on the Hill. It was impossible to find a channel that didn't have a congressman or senator standing in front of a bank of microphones, staring steely-eyed into a camera, condemning the cowardly attack upon America and swearing swift and immediate retaliation against the instigators of this horrible crime. When asked who we would retaliate against, these same politicians would stammer and stutter, grasping for a terrorist name or a certain country to blame. The smart politicians preferred not to comment and quickly moved away from the mikes. Then, there were those who saw this as a perfect chance to strengthen their political careers. Unfortunately, they only managed to demonstrate their total ignorance of the subject of terrorism by mispronouncing terrorist leaders' names and their origins. Two senators had simply made up the names of terrorist leaders who they said were responsible, and they vowed that everyone from the CIA, FBI, and Interpol knew where they could be found and an arrest was imminent. Yet another, when pressured by reporters and at a loss for the name of a terrorist country, opted for the old reliable, and blamed the whole thing on the "evil empire," Russia. The press doubted that one, but ran the film, anyway. The State Department was still trying to calm the Russian heat that resulted. The American people were in a state of confusion. Worse, they were in a state of fear. The continuous playing of the terrorist tapes sent to the radio stations served only to fan the flames of panic.

These irresponsible accusations and interviews led to a series of shootings and assaults across the nation against those nationalities that had been erroneously named in the televised reports. The country had became so engulfed in anger and fear that the president of the United States found it necessary to call a televised news conference in an attempt to calm the nation's fears. He promised that action would be taken, but emphasized the importance of pinpointing the true culprits. He asked that the people remain calm. Panic and fear served only the purpose of the terrorists. He requested the American people to toughen their resolve and not allow these murderers the benefit of disrupting the nation. He assured them that SOCOM had been hurt, but that they weren't out of the game yet.

It had been a good speech, a reassuring speech, but one that had done little to lift the heavy burden of loss and sadness that now filled the conference room. SOCOM's losses were appalling. There were 121 people killed, mostly women and children, and 156 had been wounded, thirty of whom were in critical condition and might not survive through the night. Nearly every member of the command had suffered the loss of a family member or that of a close friend. Following the immediate sense of rage, a state of deep depression and helplessness had settled over MacDill Air Force Base.

A cassette recorder sat on the table near General Johnson's arm. The tape Captain Garcia had given B.J. had already been inserted. They were waiting for Major Hatch, who had gone to the airfield to pick up Clinton Bowers, the secretary of defense, and William Rutiford Hayes, the director of the CIA. Hatch was already ten minutes late. The waiting did little to aid the silence in the room. If anything, it gave these men who craved immediate action time to think—to wonder where their loved ones were, what was happening to them right now. Time to question the actions they had taken this morning. And worst of all, time to find doubt in those decisions that each had made at critical moments.

The red phone next to General Johnson's chair rang. Answering, Johnson said, "Yes, please send them down." Replacing the receiver, he looked up at the men around the table. "Major Hatch has arrived with Mr. Bowers and Mr. Hayes," Johnson hesitated. Then, directing his attention to the men of SOCOM, he continued. "Gentlemen, I realize the tragic events of the morning have us all on edge, and that emotions and bitter feelings are running high; however, there is nothing we can do to change what has happened. We must now focus our energies on the safe recovery of our people and the elimination of those who have perpetrated this assault on America. I will remind you that Mr. Bowers is the secretary of defense and as a representative of the president of the United States, he is due the respect of that office. I expect you to conduct yourselves like the professionals you are. Do you understand?"

Without looking at the general, B.J., Jake, and Smith replied with a series of head-nodding and mumbled assurances. Johnson leaned back in his chair. Normally, he would have slammed the table with his fist, then snapped and barked for a more positive reply, but not this time. The physical and emotional stress of this morning had already taken a heavy toll on their spirits. Condemnation from him now could only add to the depression they felt, a depression from which he was not immune.

Johnson's thoughts were on Helen when the door opened and Hatch entered the room, holding the door for Secretary Clinton Bowers and William Rutiford Hayes, director of the Central Intelligence Agency. Johnson stood and waved to the two empty chairs on his right. Bowers moved to within a few feet of his old roommate from Oklahoma University. Grasping Johnson's outstretched hand tightly in his own, he said, "Jonathan, the president asked that I convey his condolences. He would have preferred to deliver that message himself, but I'm sure you have already seen the hysteria that has swept Washington. The man has his hands full. He wants you to know that SOCOM has a blank check on this one. Anything you need, just name it, and it's yours."

"Thank you, Clinton."

"Jonathan, I—I understand that Helen is one of the hostages," said Bowers.

The general averted his eyes from his friend and stared at the floor, as if ashamed. "Yes, we—we couldn't—couldn't—" Johnson's voice broke, and he fell silent.

Bowers moved closer and placed his hand on the general's shoulder as he whispered, "It's all right, Jonathan, there was nothing you could do. Don't torture yourself."

Johnson realized that all eyes in the room were on the two men. Clearing his throat abruptly, he forced his feelings aside and in his usual commanding voice said, "Gentlemen, if you will take your seats, we can proceed."

As the men were being seated, Johnson realized he hadn't spoken to the CIA director yet. Reaching across the table, he shook hands with the sixty-year-old leader of America's top intelligence agency. "Sorry, Will, didn't mean to ignore you."

"Quite all right, Jonathan, I understand," said Hayes, gripping the general's hand tightly.

Johnson remained standing until he had completed the introductions around the table. Seating himself, he pulled the cassette player in front of him.

"That, I take it, is the infamous tape that has been playing around the world all morning," said Bowers.

"Yes, it is," answered Johnson. "This particular tape was presented to Major Mattson by the terrorist leader of the helicopter assault force, a Cuban officer."

"Cuban! My God, does anyone else know that?" asked Hayes anxiously.

"No, Will, Major Mattson was the only one—other than the hostages—close enough to identify the man. No one outside of this room is aware of the nationality of any of those involved in this attack. I had the bodies of the three terrorists who were killed removed before anyone could examine them. If word got out that there were Cubans involved in this, I'm afraid we'd have an all-out war going on in the barrios of Miami right now. I thought it best we kept it quiet. We have enough problems without that. The governor of the state agreed."

Hayes turned to the lieutenant governor. "You believe it would come to that, Mr. Decord?"

"Yes, I do, sir. I'm afraid we have a number of elements within our city who would like nothing better than to use this as an excuse to burn the barrios to the ground. Anti-Hispanic feelings, especially those against the Cubans, have been running high for quite some time now. I believe the general has taken the appropriate action," said Decord.

Hayes nodded his understanding and said, "I do, too. It's amazing how quickly people forget it was the courage of a Cuban that exposed the terrorist plot to secure chemical weapons only a few short weeks ago. I'm sorry Jonathan, go ahead."

Johnson placed his finger on the play button of the cassette recorder. "I'm sure everyone has heard this tape more than once today, but I believe we should hear it again. It will give us a place to start." The room was silent as the general pressed the play button and the tape began. The deep, baritone voice of Ahmad Fisal overpowered the silence.

"People of America, I am Ahmad Fisal, commander of the forces of the Palestinian Liberation Organization and the chosen avenger of Allah. The attacks upon your citizens this morning were not the fault of the American people. The blame lies not with the people, but with their irresponsible leaders and their continued interference in the affairs of the Arab people—a people who seek only to regain their homeland, which has been stolen from them by the Jew dogs of Israel. Continued warnings to your government of the consequences of such interference has long fallen on deaf and uncaring ears.

"For those who have lost loved ones today because of that indifference to our warnings, I can only give comfort by saying to them that having served as an instrument in the holy struggle, you may be assured that they have found favor in the eyes of Allah, for they have fallen as holy warriors in his name and shall find peace eternal in his kingdom. As for the infidels who serve as the sword of Allah's tormentors, let the actions of this day serve notice that no longer shall they be permitted to interfere with impunity in the causes of valiant freedom fighters of the world without suffering the same fate as those who they so ruthlessly seek to destroy. They call us terrorists, yet through clandestine operations, they illegally infiltrate countries, conduct kidnappings, commit assassinations, and, like pirates, openly fire on ships on the open seas—all in the name of national security. I would ask you, which is the terrorist, and which the freedom fighter?"

There was a slight pause in the tape. Someone could be heard speaking in the background. It was barely audible, but it sounded like a woman's voice. There was the muffled sound of Fisal saying something, then a ten-second silence before Fisal began again. Hayes made a note on the pad in front of him as Fisal continued.

"For too long now, the Jew-loving politicians of America have allowed their mercenaries to roam the world at will, striking out with their great power without fear of retaliation; but now, your judgment has come, and I, Ahmad Fisal, have been chosen as the almighty arm of Allah to seek out and do battle with the evil arm of the Great Satan. However, Allah is all merciful, he has no desire to bring death to the innocent. The actions of this morning were necessary so that we might bring our challenge before the world for all to see. We seek only those who have sinned against Allah. It is for that reason that we have found it necessary to secure twenty-five of your fellow Americans as our guests. They are being held in an isolated area referred to as the Big Cypress Swamp, in the Everglades of the state you call Florida. It is at this place the great battle between good and evil will be played out. It is not our intention, nor the wish of Allah that further innocents be harmed. They are but the beacon with which to draw from hiding the evil arm of the Great Satan and force him to do battle. The battle shall proceed much as a game. A game in which the true evil shall fall from grace and be exposed for all to see.

"Who are these antagonists in the service of the Great Satan, you ask? They are the unholy leaders of your Special Operations Command—murderers for hire who are funded by your CIA. They follow the orders of the corrupt leaders of your country who would visit war and terror upon your land. They are ambitious men, who boast openly of the murder and mayhem they have spread among innocents of other countries. It is these men who we seek: General J. J. Johnson, the so-called commander of this pack of dogs; Major B. J. Mattson, a criminal of the Vietnam War, who serves as a lackey for his commander; the final murderer to face his fate is also a servant of the devil Johnson. His name is Lieutenant Commander Jacob Mortimer, a man of power and wealth who serves only to kill for his pleasure. These are the true enemies of Allah, and the ones responsible for the misery many have suffered this day. They are the chosen challengers.

"The three infidels shall each be permitted to select one other murderer to join forces with them. These six shall then be pitted against my forces, consisting of only seven men and three women. Surely, men of such reputed prowess in weapons and warfare should be more than a match for ten fanatical terrorists."

"Bullshit!" said Hayes, rocking forward in his chair and pulling a stubby cigar from his lips. "The bastard has at least thirty damn people in there. The asshole has already stacked the deck."

Johnson stopped the tape and now said, "We know that, Will, but would the world believe us or Fisal? We go in there with more than six men, and a lot of people are going to wonder if maybe this son of a bitch isn't right about a lot of things."

"Sorry, Jonathan," said Hayes, leaning back in his chair. "Go ahead. The bastard's almost finished, anyway. Let's get this over with so we can start planning a way to hand Mr. Ahmad Fisal his balls."

B.J. and Jake grinned at one another, then winked at the fiery old director. They liked that idea. Johnson punched the play button once more.

"The battleground will be an area ten miles square. The coordinates of the four corners have been printed on this tape. The guests have been confined in a structure directly in the center of this area. Two hundred pounds of plastic explosives surround the structure. These explosives can be detonated by remote control. Miniature radar units have been placed at various locations within the battle area and can be monitored at our main base. The approach of any aircraft into this area will result in the immediate death of the prisoners. High-frequency and heat-generated sensors are similarly located around the perimeter of this battle area. Any penetration of this zone by any other than the designated team of Americans who have been selected to represent the Special Operations Command, will result in the death of the prisoners.

"I would caution you to utilize all of the power and influence at your command to make sure that neither of these rules is violated by 'unfortunate accidents' committed by overzealous intruders. Keeping those not involved in the game from this area is your responsibility. We will not be understanding, nor will we allow for accidents. We will simply detonate our explosives and fade away to strike another day. Their deaths shall be on your heads, and the world will know that it was your violation of the challenge that led to those deaths, not ours. The game will begin at dawn tomorrow. It is a simple game. Once the chosen men have crossed our sensors and entered the battle area, they have only to reach the site where the prisoners are being held and release them to win both the game and the freedom of your fellow citizens. Should they fail in their attempt, they will sacrifice the lives of the prisoners. The world will see that these murderers who serve their political masters rather than their god, have unjustly been portrayed as heroes, when in fact they are no more than cold, calculating killers, whose fame has spread throughout this land through the killing of women, old men, and children. They will not be dealing with old men or children this time tomorrow. We shall see who is vindicated in the eyes of their god.

"Should fate intervene and both sides lose, the prisoners

will all perish. This is only fitting, as it will be a sign that both gods have turned away from their followers. Therefore, a timing device has been placed with the detonators. It will be activated once the sun has broken the horizon in the morning. Having spent many hours studying your Holy Bible, I have selected a time frame I believe to be appropriate. For forty days and forty nights, your god cast a rain upon the earth. In the end, only the faithful survived. So shall it be with the twenty-five we now hold. You shall have forty hours in which to rescue your faithful. We shall expect you at dawn. Praise be to Allah, the all powerful."

Turning the recorder off, Johnson looked around the table. "There you have it, gentlemen. We know the rules; we know the place, and we know when the game begins. What we need now is a game plan. I suggest we begin by finding out just where we are so far. The president has given us carte blanche on this operation. Mr. Hayes, could you bring us up to date, please?"

Will Hayes removed a folder from his briefcase, placed it in front of him, flipped it open, and began, "Of course, General, but I'm afraid it's not a pretty picture. We are seriously lacking in our intelligence on terrorists movements over the past few months. What happened this morning is a direct result of that shortcoming. Our boy Ahmad Fisal is one of the heavyweights in the terrorist business, totally committed to the Palestinian cause and totally ruthless in his methods of achieving the organization's goals. From what we can piece together from cross-referencing intelligence from our Israeli friends and Interpol, Fisal has been engineering this operation for over three months."

"Well, I'll be goddamned!" said Sergeant Smith loudly. "Just where the fuck were you guys all this time?" Turning his rage toward Dan Hampton, he shouted, "Where the fuck was the FBI? You guys are supposed to be the hotshots at nailing assholes like this sneaking into this damn country. Just what the hell were you doin' for three goddamn months, huh? Hidin' in some fuckin' corner, jackin' each other off?"

The outcry stunned everyone in the room. Hampton, the FBI man, jumped to his feet. "Now, just a minute here. I don't have—"

B.J. reached over and clasped his longtime friend's arm. "Easy, Tommy." Looking across at Hayes and Hampton, he said, "Gentlemen, Sergeant Smith's wife and two children are among the hostages. Mine as well. I believe you can understand the strain we're under here."

The news hit the FBI man hard. Slowly lowering himself back into his chair, he whispered, "I'm—I'm sorry, Sergeant Smith. I didn't know."

Tommy had vented his rage, and now he felt exhausted. "No, I'm the one that should apologize. Yellin' at you ain't goin' to do any good. I'm sorry."

General Johnson was on the verge of having Smith leave the room. If he hadn't apologized when he did, he would have been gone. Turning to a sad-eyed Hayes, Johnson said, "Go on, Will."

Hayes avoided looking directly at either Mattson or Smith as he continued. "The Palestinians infiltrated through Cuba. Major Mattson's positive identification of the Cuban officer confirms that theory. Obviously, Fidel infiltrated a Cuban Special Forces pathfinder team into Florida in advance of Fisal's arrival."

Jake sat up in his chair. "So, what we've got is a repeat of our last mission—a joint Arab-Cuban operation."

"Not quite, Commander Mortimer," replied Dan Hampton. "We've already started a workup on the three terrorists who were killed this morning. We sent prints and dental tracers on all three to Interpol. We received positive ID on two of them. They were both Germans involved with what remains of the old Baader-Meinhof gang. They were last reported in South America. The third was definitely an Arab. We should have his name soon."

Hayes stared over at B.J. and asked, "Major, did you notice anyone else besides the Cuban?"

"Yeah, as a matter of fact, I did. There was a little Oriental guy there, too. I was about to blow his brains out when the Cuban showed up. They called him Komura, or something like that. They only said his name once, but I remember it sounded awfully familiar. I was a little too busy to think about it at the time."

"Are you sure it wasn't Imura?" asked Hayes.

"Oh, hell," sighed Jake. "The leader of the Avenging Sun group. The terrorist outfit that pulled off the three hits on three airports at the same time."

"That's where I've heard the name before," said B.J., slumping back in his chair. "Looks like we've got an international terrorist convention in town, and we're scheduled to be the guests of honor."

"Okay," said Johnson, "Will, is it possible that Fisal could have that area as wired as he says he does with radar, sensors, and all the high-tech equipment necessary to monitor it?"

Hayes pulled a piece of paper from his folder. "Three months is a long time to prepare, Jonathan. I'm afraid it is very possible that he does. This is a report from Reimhosen, Germany. A little over two months ago, one of the NATO warehouses was broken into. Among the items stolen were six of the new miniature radar systems and twenty-four heat sensors."

"Christ," mumbled Smith under his breath. "You know he already has that crap in place out there. He don't sound like the kinda boy that bullshits a whole lot. Know what I mean? You can bet he's not kiddin' about blowing those hostages to hell and back."

"I won't lie to you, Jonathan. If you go through with this thing, you're looking at going up against thirty, maybe forty guns out there," said Hayes. "There's no way six of you could possibly reach the hostages against those kinds of odds. I suggest we mount a parachute assault into the area and establish blocking forces on all four sides. We'll nail them as they try to escape."

The suggestion met with steely glares from the members of SOCOM, Johnson included. "No way, Mr. Hayes. I'm not about to write off twenty-five of my people that easily. I don't care if the bastard's got a hundred and forty other assholes out there with him. We don't give up that easily around here." Pausing, Johnson looked down the table at the lieutenant governor. "Mr. Decord, can the governor halt all air traffic over that area? I mean everything? I don't even want a 747 at fifty thousand feet crossing that square. Can you arrange that?"

"We can certainly try, General. I may need Mr. Bowers's help and authority, but I'm sure we can do it."

"Very well," said Johnson, turning to Major Hatch. "Erin, have you plotted the coordinates Fisal gave on the tape?"

"Yes, sir, my staff is setting up the charts and maps in the operations room at this time. I have ordered hourly weather reports and nighttime illumination percentages. We'll have a quarter moon to work with tomorrow night."

Hayes and the other civilians in the room sat silently in disbelief, listening as plans were made to accommodate Fisal and his sadistic terrorist game. They were going to do it—six men were going to attempt what, in the minds of these civilians, was little more than suicide. They envied the courage of these men of SOCOM, but even they had little chance against six- or seven-to-one odds. Hayes realized mentioning that point would do little good. The challenge had been put forth and accepted by Johnson and the others. The determination in their eyes and the seriousness in their faces as Johnson spoke left no doubt of where they planned to be at dawn tomorrow.

"Erin, get in touch with NASA Central. I want satellite coverage of every inch of the battle area. Have them fax the photos as soon as they have them. While you're waiting, I want you to contact the National Forestry boys in Miami. I want everything they've got on the Big Cypress waterways; old ones, new ones, any proposed ones they haven't even started yet. Depth, width, everything and anything you can come up with. You got it?"

"Yes, sir, I've got it," said Hatch, rushing out of the room.

An air of excitement began to spread around the room as Johnson's confident voice reeled off orders. "Clinton, you and Mr. Decord had better get started on our aircraft problem. I imagine that's going to take a lot of time and cause the biggest headache. Stress the fact that these people we are dealing with are hard-core killers—they don't bluff. One plane crosses that A.O. and the terrorists will blow those hostages off the face of this earth. Make them understand that, Clinton."

The secretary and lieutenant governor were on their feet. The earlier feeling of helplessness was replaced now by one of determined purpose. With each new directive, the general's voice strengthened and showed new life. Bowers smiled to himself. This was the General J. J. Johnson he knew: tough, confident, and positive.

"Okay, Jonathan, if they don't want to cooperate the easy way, then by God, I'll have the president declare martial law and government troops will take over the airports until this thing is over."

"I'll hold you to that, Mr. Secretary," said Johnson with a grin.

Bowers slapped his old friend on the shoulder. Then he and Mr. Decord left. They had a lot of phone calls to make.

At the far end of the table, B.J., Jake, and Tommy Smith were studying a map of the Everglades. Johnson joined them.

"First impressions, gentlemen?" he asked.

B.J. answered, "It's going to be a real bitch, sir. They've got those damn sensors, and you know they'll have them spread throughout the area, not just the perimeter of the battle area. They'll be able to track our general direction of movement and have plenty of time to set up ambushes anywhere along the way."

"Yeah," said Jake, "if not an ambush, booby traps, for sure."

"This boy's a right smart fellow, General," said Smith. "He knew exactly what he was doing when he came up with the rules. He sets the number we can have at six. We try using any of our fancy heat reflection decoy systems, we're screwed. Anything that comes up on his sensor detectors that shows more than six warm bodies, and the hostages have had it. He's figured a long time on this thing, no doubt about it."

General Johnson ran his fingers through his snow-white hair and sat on the edge of the table as he said, "I agree with all three of you, gentlemen. It would appear that the odds are all in his favor and that he has the perfect plan." There was a moment's pause; then, "Therein lies his weakness."

The three men glanced at one another, then to the general.

"Excuse me, sir," said B.J., "but did we miss something here? What weakness?"

Johnson cracked a smile as he replied, "Hell, gentlemen, we all know there is no such thing as the perfect plan. It goes against nature. There has to be a flaw in Fisal's plan. All we have to do is find it. And damn it, gentlemen, if we can't find it, no one can. Are you ready to go to work?"

"Airborne, sir!" said Smith.

"Right on!" cried Jake.

"What the hell. Only one guy ever walked the earth with the perfect plan, and he had it figured right down to the hanging on the cross. Fisal isn't that good. Let's get on it," said B.J.

William R. Hayes had observed the high-spirited pep rally from across the room. As Johnson and his men moved toward the door to leave, he asked, "General, excuse me, sir, but what kind of help do you want from the agency?"

"No interference," snapped Johnson, who immediately realized that the remark sounded harsher than he had intended. "Sorry, Will, I didn't mean for that to come out that way, but I know how your CIA boys like to jump into the middle of things sometimes, and they don't always land on their feet. What I mean to say is, if this operation gets screwed up and turns to shit, we'd rather it be our fault. I hope you understand."

The CIA director's face held a look of disappointed rejection, but he understood. All of the hostages were SOCOM people. They were family. If this thing went down wrong, Johnson didn't want it to be because of a mistake caused by an outsider.

"Okay, Jonathan, you're calling the shots. One thing I would like to do though—we've got a new toy in our arsenal. The boys up at the CIA training farm call it 'Big

Dick.' It's a reinforced armilite rifle with a kevlar buffer and a torqued recoil spring. It only weighs fifteen pounds."

"Jesus!" exclaimed Smith. "What's it fire, a fuckin' fifty caliber slug?"

"Exactly," said Hayes with a deadpan expression.

B.J. looked at the general for a second, then back to Hayes. "No disrespect, sir, but after firing one shot from a cannon like that, a guy's shoulder would be numb for an hour."

Hayes shook his head. "No, Major Mattson. The special shoulder pad attached to the stock is more than sufficient to counter the shock of the recoil. We've been test-firing the weapon for over three weeks now. Some of the men have fired as many as two hundred rounds in a day with no aftereffects. It has proven to be deadly accurate and devastatingly effective. At a distance of four hundred yards, it can penetrate completely through a tree six feet in diameter, and a four-foot-thick brick wall at three hundred yards."

The impressive statistics brought another round of silence from the group. Johnson saw B.J. was considering the weapon. He cast a raised eyebrow at the major and shrugged his shoulders. If he wanted to use it, he was welcome to. It was Jake Mortimer who spoke up first. "Oh, what the hell! We're already going to have six suicidal dicks out there. What's one more? I'll carry the damn thing. Who knows? I might just come across a *Tyrannosaurus rex* out there."

"A what?" asked Smith.

"A dinosaur, Tommy," said B.J.

"Yeah, right!" said Smith dryly.

The sound of laughter was heard for the first time that afternoon as the members of SOCOM departed the conference room and headed for the operations section. Hayes left to coordinate the shipment of the weapon to MacDill.

Erin Hatch came running down the hallway and called to the general just as they were about to enter operations.

"Easy, son," said Johnson as Hatch pulled up short of the door. "What is it, Erin? Not more bad news, I hope."

The intelligence office caught his breath, then replied, "Well, sir, that depends on one's perspective, I guess."

"Well, what is it, son?"

Hatch was trying hard to maintain a straight face. "Sir, we've checked everywhere—the beach, the park, the quarters, and every damn place on base—but, we still couldn't find him."

"Who can't we find, Major?" asked Johnson.

"General Sweet, sir. We believe he is one of the hostages."

B.J. couldn't help but snicker, and Jake and Smith began to laugh. The general started to reprimand them, then found himself smiling. True, it was hardly a laughing matter, yet one had to appreciate the ironic twist of fate. The very men that General Raymond Sweet had struggled so desperately to destroy for the past two years were now all that stood between him and his maker.

CHAPTER 8

Charlotte Mattson and Nancy Smith sat on the damp ground in a corner of the barbed-wire pen that surrounded the small island on which they and the other hostages had been placed. A swamp-water moat ten yards wide completely surrounded the small hump of ground and separated them from the terrorist base camp.

Nancy removed the last cigarette from her pack. Cursing under her breath, she crumpled up the empty pack and tossed it to the ground. Searching for her lighter, she once again answered the same question that Charlotte had been asking her repeatedly.

"Yes, Charlotte, B.J. was fine, I told you. They didn't do anything to him. They could have, but they didn't. The Cuban guy showed up and they talked for a few minutes, then B.J. let the Oriental guy go, and that was it. He was just sitting there on the ground when we lifted off, but he wasn't hurt."

Charlotte pointed to the lighter that had fallen from Nancy's purse and lay half hidden behind her. She said,

"God, this is going to sound morbid, but I wonder why they didn't kill him? I mean, they were shooting at everybody else. You'd think a military man in uniform would be a primary target—especially an American officer."

Nancy lit her precious last cigarette, inhaled deeply, and blew the smoke out through her nose. "Hell, who can say with these assholes? To them, shooting Americans is a recreational sport. Maybe fatigues were out of season this morning. Christ, Charlotte, I don't know—I just don't know."

Charlotte heard the biting tension in her friend's voice. It was a tone brought on by an inner struggle that balanced precariously between courage and fear. Nancy was a strong-willed person, something Charlotte had always admired in the woman. If it were just her they were holding, she could deal with this, but it wasn't just her. There were the kids. Her fear was more out of concern for them than for herself.

Staring silently across the way, Charlotte watched the older children playing games with the younger ones in an effort to take their minds off the situation.

"I can't believe these people think they can get away with this," said Charlotte quietly. "You saw all the planes circling overhead when we landed in that field this morning. Our people have to know where we are."

Nancy let a curl of smoke slip its way from her lips as she turned her head skyward. "There's more to this thing than just a simple kidnapping, Charlotte."

"What do you mean, Nancy?"

"Well, these terrorists didn't seem at all worried about all that commotion going on overhead when we set down in that field. Hell, they even had a landing party in plain sight popping smoke and directing the landings. It was like they knew our people couldn't do anything to them. Did you notice how high our fighters were? They only circled. They didn't make one low-level pass—not one. And now look—not a plane in the sky. No fighters, no choppers, not even a damn commercial airliner, and Florida has about as much air traffic as L.A., but not today."

Charlotte tilted her head back and searched the skies. Nancy was right. If not military aircraft, there should at least be a commercial airliner or a private plane crossing the heavens every now and then, but the sky was void of anything but an occasional flight of birds rising out of the swamps and making their way silently across the clear blue sky. "Whe-when did you first notice that, Nancy?"

Nancy smashed out the cigarette and replied, "About an hour ago. Once they escorted us off the LZ and destroyed the helicopters, our fighters just disappeared. I kept listening as they were moving us through the swamp. I actually expected to hear flights of helicopters coming in for an airmobile assault or something dramatic. I've been listening ever since, but nothing—not a damn thing. It's like everyone outside these friggin' swamps just called it a day and went home. It's creepy, honey, real creepy."

Jason Mattson and Troy Smith came over and sat down beside their mothers. There was a look of seriousness in their faces. Their eyes were intense. "Mom," said Jason, "we don't want to scare you, but we thought you should know—you see those men digging outside the fence?"

Charlotte didn't feel comfortable with her son's tone of voice. She was not really sure she wanted to know what he had to say. "Yes, Jason, why? What's wrong?"

The two boys stared across at each other for a long moment. Troy nodded his head. "Might as well go ahead and tell them, Jason."

"What are you two talking about, Troy?" asked Nancy.

"They're—they're placing explosives all around us, Mom," said Jason. "Lots of it."

"Yeah," chimed in Troy. "Enough to make this little piece of ground disappear in one big flash and bang."

The two women sat in silence. Their gaze was fixed on the men outside the wire. The color seemed to fade from Charlotte Mattson's face as she whispered, "Oh, my God, they intend to kill us after all, no matter what happens."

Nancy placed a hand on Charlotte's arm to calm her. Then, looking at her son, she asked, "Troy, are you sure about this?"

"Yeah, Mom, I'm afraid so. You remember that piece of white play-dough looking stuff that Dad brought home once? It's called C-4. It's a plastic explosive. Comes in long one-pound blocks. That's what those rag-heads are planting out there, and not just blocks, but cases of the crap."

"Nancy, what are we going to do?" asked Charlotte, her voice on the edge of panic as tears began to fill her eyes.

Nancy wrapped her arm around Charlotte. She could feel her friend trembling. "Now, don't you worry. Like they say, the game ain't over till the fat lady sings, and I believe that. You know B.J., Tommy, Jake, the general—all of 'em—are working on getting us out of this mess. You know I'm right, Charlotte. So don't let this get to you. Our guys have dealt with situations like this before. They can handle it. You just hang in there. I've got a feeling this thing is just getting warmed up." Turning to the two boys, Nancy said, "Have either of you told anyone else about this?"

Both shook their heads, signaling that they hadn't.

"Good. Don't. The last thing we need right now is a panic. The children are still scared, but are handling it pretty well, now. We need to keep it that way. You two go on back and join the others. Don't say anything, okay?"

The boys nodded and returned to the group of kids. Helen Cantrell waited until the boys had walked away, then approached the two women at the fence. "Would you mind if I joined you?" she asked.

Charlotte looked up. "Of course, Helen, please do."

Helen sat down beside them.

"We were just discussing our situation, Helen. I told Charlotte I was sure ol' Q-Tip—uh—General Johnson—and the others were already working on a plan to put an end to this," Nancy said.

"She's right, Charlotte. I don't think we will be here long. Not if I know Jonathan and your husband as well as I think I do. They'll know how to deal with these terrorists, and it will be soon. You can count on it," said Helen, placing a reassuring hand on Charlotte's arm. "We just have to be brave and stick together until then."

Nancy was about to agree with Helen, when suddenly, a man's voice cried out, "Hey! What are you doing there? They're planting explosives! They're going to blow us up!"

Some of the women began to scream. Children ran to their mothers, crying and screaming. The few men who had been taken hostage ran to the fence where the man was still screaming and pointing at the cases of plastic explosives. Their angry voices joined in the protest. The cries rose to such a level that Fisal and Mueller came out of the headquarters to see what all the commotion was about. Imura came up to them and explained that one of the hostages had seen the C-4 and his cries had started a panic among the hostages. The screaming, shouting, and crying, which were increasing by the second, were proving irritable to Fisal.

"Mueller, handle that. I want them quiet. I have no time for the whining of frightened sheep."

The German flashed a sadistic smile, clicked his heels together, then walked toward the small log bridge that spanned the moat. Eva and two of the Palestinians joined him.

"Uh oh," whispered Nancy, "there's going to be trouble. We have to get the kids and the other women away from the fence." Helen, Charlotte, and Nancy jumped to their feet and began rounding everyone up and moving them to a far corner of the stockade. It was then that Nancy noticed the man who had started the panic. He was slowly backing away from the fence and filtering to the back of the crowd. He was wearing the ugliest shirt she'd ever seen and a pair of ill-fitting Bermuda shorts.

The other men at the wire were directing their attention to the approaching group led by Mueller, and did not take notice of the man's departure. Nancy turned to Charlotte and asked, "Charlotte, isn't that man coming this way General Sweet?"

Charlotte studied his face as the man approached. "I—I think it is, Nancy. I'm not sure, I've only met him—"

"It is General Sweet," said Helen, with a hint of disgust in her voice. "I should have known he would be behind this trouble. Jonathan says that in any hierarchy, each individual rises to his own level of incompetence, and remains there. Sweet is a perfect example of that."

Sweet stood only five feet six, and right now, his little legs were carrying him swiftly toward the safety of the women and children. His overweight frame jiggled about like Jell-O under his purple-and-orange Hawaiian shirt. Sweat formed along his forehead and trickled down his chubby cheeks. Fear was clearly visible in his beady black eyes. He reached the women just as Mueller stepped to the wire to confront the men at the wire. The shouting died down for a moment as words were exchanged between the German and the hostages.

Nancy was about to chastise Sweet for causing this problem, when Helen suddenly gasped, "My word, who is that young woman? Isn't that the girl Jake has been dating?"

Beverly Mills was standing only a few yards to the right of the men at the fence. She had a small camera in her hands and was busy clicking frame after frame of the confrontation.

"Yes, that's Beverly Mills, the reporter from CNN News," said Charlotte.

"She won't be dating anybody, Mom, if she doesn't put that camera away and get away from that fence," said Jason Mattson.

"I'll go get her," said Troy Smith, moving forward a couple of steps before his mother grabbed him.

"Like hell you will. You're staying right here."

"Aw, Mom, I—"

A series of shots rang out. Everyone dropped to the ground. There were more shots as the male hostages at the fence turned to run for cover. Beverly Mills had dropped to the ground as well, but was still clicking the camera, photographing the bodies of the three dead Americans that lay only a few scant yards away. A fourth lay in the middle of the stockade with two holes in his back and blood slowly spreading across his shirt.

"Hold your fire!" screamed Major Ruiz, as he and Fisal came running across the bridge. "Stop firing, god damn it!"

Mueller was replacing his pistol in his holster as Fisal stepped to within inches of the German's face. Grating his teeth in frustration, he growled, "I said to keep them quiet, you fool, not kill them."

Mueller didn't back away. His eyes were stone cold as

he laughed, "I am not known for my diplomacy, Herr Fisal. You wanted me to handle it, so I did—my way. Do you hear any of them whining now? I rest my case."

For a fleeting second, Fisal considered ridding himself of this man once and for all. Mueller's egocentric attitude could only lead to further problems later when obedience to orders would become critical. It was only the sudden frantic outburst from Eva Schmidt that temporarily removed the idea. The blond Amazon was shouting in German and pointing to Beverly Mills and her camera. Fisal motioned, and two Palestinians rushed inside the wire and jerked the woman to her feet. Tossing the camera over the wire to Major Ruiz, they awaited orders from Fisal as to what to do with her. Fisal stepped closer to the fence. He had seen this woman somewhere before; he was sure of it. He was trying to recall where, as he openly admired her young, well-built body. One of the guards held her arms pinned behind her back. The nipples of her firm, rounded breasts were clearly visible through the tightly drawn nylon tank top. It was a tantalizing view that did not go unnoticed by Eva Schmidt, who slowly ran her tongue over her lips as she, too, stared at the breasts and the smooth exposed skin of the woman's stomach.

"What is your name, woman?" asked Fisal softly.

"Beverly Mills," she replied, a little frightened by his lustful glare.

"Oh, yes, that is where I have seen that face. You are a reporter, are you not?"

"Yes—I—I work for CNN News," answered Beverly, who suddenly thought of escape. "I could help you, you know."

"Oh, really. How might you do that, Miss Mills?"

"CNN coverage is worldwide. I could arrange for you to broadcast your story exclusively around the world. Millions

would see you. You could have an open forum to the world
from which to air your grievances and explain your cause.
If you were to release me, I could bring a crew back here.
We could transmit from here, if you like. We could be set
up before dark."

Fisal studied her eyes as she spoke. He saw the desperation there and was not fooled by her promises.

"Fisal, surely you have no intentions of releasing this
bitch," said Mueller. "She only seeks a way out of here.
She won't even think of returning if you let her go. Besides,
she knows four of the hostages have been killed. That
would be her big story, not why we are here."

Fisal's eyes roamed over her body once more, the slow
rising and falling of her breasts as she breathed, the deeply
tanned legs and tight-fitting shorts. Major Ruiz saw the look
in the Arab's eyes, and recognized it for what it was: pure,
unadulterated lust. True, the woman was desirable, but this
was neither the place nor the time. It would be dark soon.
They now had less than four hours to make final preparations for the arrival of Johnson and his men at dawn. Yet,
none of this seemed to bother Fisal. Ruiz failed to see why
his Cubans and Imura were the only participants in this
operation who took the men of SOCOM seriously. They
were only six men, perhaps, but they were not typical
soldiers. They were going to prove harder to handle than
Fisal and the others thought.

Captain Garcia had told Ruiz of meeting B. J. Mattson
and of the fiery glare in the eyes of the American when he
gave him the tape. The look had sent a shiver down the
young Cuban officer's spine. It had been as if he had found
himself staring into the eyes of the devil himself. Garcia
had openly admitted it had frightened him. Only by lying
and telling Captain Garcia that he had freed the young
captives who Fisal had arrived with, was Ruiz able to take

the captain's thoughts off Mattson and those eyes. The devil was coming at dawn, and all Fisal had on his mind was getting laid.

"You may have an excellent point, Miss Mills. Unfortunately, Herr Mueller is correct. I cannot allow you to leave. However, I am willing to compromise. Could you make the required arrangements by radio?" asked Fisal.

Both Mueller and Ruiz started to protest. Fisal raised his hand quickly and shouted, "Silence!"

Although frightened by this man, Beverly was still harboring the thought of escape. Her chances were better outside the wire. She answered, "Yes, I suppose I could arrange it."

A polite, almost fatherly smile crossed the Arab's face as he said, "Fine, then, come along. I have a radio in my quarters. We will contact your people and give them our suggestions."

Fisal waved for his men to release her. They followed her out the gate, where she joined Fisal. They all walked toward his quarters. Fisal and the young woman went inside. The two guards posted themselves at each side of the door. Mueller's look of protest had vanished. It was replaced by a wide, toothy grin. Major Ruiz ordered some of the men to remove the dead from the stockade, then he walked away.

Mueller and Eva whispered back and forth as they crossed the bridge, then they broke out in laughter. Captain Garcia joined Major Ruiz and asked, "What do you think those two degenerates found so funny?"

Major Ruiz never broke stride as he said, "There are no radios in Fisal's quarters." As they passed Fisal's door, they heard the woman's muffled scream and the sound of cloth being torn. Garcia hesitated. The major ordered him to keep moving. As they started into the swamp, Garcia looked back. Eva Schmidt lit a cigarette and peered through the cracks of the makeshift hut, finding satisfaction in observing the rape that was taking place. She didn't think Fisal would take long. Then it would be her turn to play with the little girl with the great body.

CHAPTER 9

The beer and liquor were flowing freely at Cully's Place. Red Culder, the owner, hadn't done this much business since the New Year's bash. Outraged rednecks and bitter hard cases swallowed their booze and cussed everyone from Arabs to Hispanics. Someone had even started a rumor that it was "them damn Florida niggers" who had helped sneak the terrorists into the country. Boastful talk and drunken threats were the order of the day. The combination of alcohol and men struggling to shout above their own fears was slowly creating a deadly situation.

One of the local toughs was a big, burly man named Marcus Taylor. Over the years, Taylor had enticed more than a few free drinks from the patrons of Cully's Place with his tales of his daring deeds while serving as a sniper in Vietnam. He envisioned himself as Florida's own Rambo. Looking up, Taylor saw the words "Special Bulletin" appear on the TV screen above the bar. "Hey! You shitheads, listen up! Shut up goddamn it! They got more news comin' over the tube. Quiet, and let's listen."

A murmured silence swept over the crowded barroom as all eyes turned to the familiar face that appeared on the screen. "Good evening, this is Dan Rather with a special news bulletin. The events that have besieged our nation on this infamous day will be addressed by the president of the United States, who will speak to the nation one hour from now. The address will be carried live by all television and radio stations across the land. We have confirmed that all air traffic, both military and civilian, has been curtailed from entering the air space over the southern portion of Florida. This precaution is in compliance with terrorist threats to the estimated twenty-five men, women, and children taken hostage during this morning's massacre at Gadsden Point. The White House has asked that the American people remain calm. Proper authorities are still evaluating the taped demands of the terrorist group and plan to announce a course of action within the next few hours."

The newsman appeared tired and tense as he paused, set his papers aside, and stared directly into the camera. A sadness surrounded his words as he said, "We, at CBS, wish to express our heartfelt sorrow to our fellow newsmen and women at CNN for the losses they suffered while covering the events at the SOCOM ceremonies this morning. We have just received a copy of the last tape shot by Darrin Evers, a CNN cameraman who was on the scene the moment the attack occurred. Mr. Evers was one of those killed this morning. I have been informed that this film is highly graphic and may prove too disturbing for some of our viewers."

The screen flashed from Dan Rather to the tape that had been recorded by Beverly Mills's cameraman during the attack. It was the most shocking and breathtaking piece of film to be broadcast since the days of the Vietnam War. First, there was Beverly Mills, microphone in hand, stating that the ceremonies were about to begin. The camera suddenly wavered and swung away from the newswoman to the beach. Sounds of gunfire and screams were clearly audible as people scrambled in all directions. The camera-man moved closer and caught the sounds and pictures of death as people along the beach were cut down by the terrorists.

There was total silence in the bar as the men watched the camera suddenly begin a wild shaking movement as the terrorists moved toward the camera. The pictures bounced about, showing sand, then sky, then sand again. The cameraman was obviously running, trying to get away from the oncoming onslaught. He didn't make it. There were the sounds of weapons fire, then a dull thud, a moan, and the camera went flying through the air, end over end, coming to rest on its side in the sand. Ironically, the camera landed in such a manner that it recorded the final moments of its owner's life. Bloody, and trying to crawl away, the cam-eraman glanced directly into the camera. A pair of boots suddenly appeared beside him. The loud sound of automatic weapons fire could be heard. The all-seeing camera re-corded every bullet as they struck the helpless man and jerked him about in the sand like a rag doll. The scene brought a low moan from the barroom patrons.

Dan Rather sat perfectly still; his eyes still staring down at the small monitor in front of him. He was visibly shaken by what he had just witnessed, as was the nation. From off camera somewhere, there was a muttering of concerned voices. Rather stared up at the camera, his eyes still rejecting what he had just seen. "We—we will keep you updated on the latest developments as they occur." The famed reporter started to say something else, but the words wouldn't come out. Waving the off signal, he jumped to his feet and left the desk. The screen went black for a moment. The "Special Bulletin" sign appeared again as another voice said, "This has been a CBS News bulletin."

Red Culder pressed the remote and lowered the sound of the commercial advertisement for Sony Camcorders. A haunting silence hung over the bar. Men were still running the vision of Darrin Evers's murder through their alcohol-soaked minds. Finally, someone yelled, "Goddamn rag-heads! What are we waiting for? Hell, those bastards ain't hiding more than ten miles from here. Let them fuckin' politicians sit on their ass and think about what to do. That's all they ever do, anyway. But we don't have to. Shit, we got Marcus, here, who can teach them damn terrorists a thing or two. Ain't that right, Marcus?"

The comment brought a riotous round of cheers from the men in the bar. Red Culder reached across the bar and slapped Taylor on the back as he joined in, "Goddamn right, he can. What do you say, Marcus? Let's go out there and kick some ass on them boys and get our folks back."

Taylor stood with his back to the bar, enjoying the cheers and hearing his name shouted in admiration. "Hell, why not?"

This brought another round of cheers and free drinks on the house. Lifting his glass of Jack Daniel's and smiling at his willing followers, Taylor downed his drink in one shot. No one around him would have guessed the trembling that was going on in the big man's gut. He knew something they didn't. In the three years he had served in the Army, he had never seen Vietnam. Marcus Taylor had not gotten beyond the Fort Dix stockade, and his dishonorable discharge was never mentioned.

As Red poured him another drink, the self-made hero thought of the position in which he had now placed himself.

Hell, he had done a lot of hunting in his time, and besides, most of these ol' boys had been going into those swamps after gators for years. They knew every inch of ground. All he had to do was be in charge. Taylor had told his stories for so long that he himself had begun to believe them. That and the alcohol was all it took. Slamming his glass down on the bar, he climbed up on a chair and yelled, "Okay! Listen up! It'll be gettin' dark soon. I want every man that is a true American to go get your guns and meet me and Red at Ford's Crossing. Bring plenty of ammunition and any extra guns you have for those that don't have none. We'll go in after them assholes after dark and surprise the shit out of them damn terrorists, then kill every one of the bastards, and bring them hostages outta there. Now, get outta here. We'll meet at the crossin' in one hour."

The effects of the news tape and the alcohol had made them all willing participants in the proposed scheme. Within minutes, Red Culder and Marcus Taylor were the only two men left in the bar. Red was as patriotic as the next guy, but now, looking around at the empty bar, he realized that a lot of money had just walked out those doors. Pouring them both another round, he suggested that it might be a better idea to wait until morning. They could bring the boys back here and plan their strategy. Taylor was drunk, but he wasn't stupid. He knew exactly why Red wanted them back here. Tossing down his drink, he pushed the glass back over to Culder. Grinning, he said, "Hey, Red, don't worry 'bout it. We'll have them rag-heads deader than dog shit and be back here drinkin' before midnight. Matter of fact, you're gonna come out of this pretty good. Your place'll become a damn national monument. You'll have to build it out another three hundred feet just to make room for the crowds."

Red poured another round. "You really think so, Marcus?"

"Hell, yes. People will come from everywhere to see the men who stood up for America against these terrorist assholes. And they'll wanta meet the man that led them." Taylor paused. Looking over the top of his glass at Culder, he said, "Red, you ever give much thought to having a partner?"

CHAPTER 10

The operations room was bustling with activity as intelligence updates were marked and posted. Material about a number of the terrorists was coming in from around the world. The German government had faxed photos of all known living members of the Baader-Meinhof gang. Israeli intelligence had done the same and included a rather hefty file on Ahmad Fisal. Information on the Oriental and the so-called Avenging Sun element of the terrorist group was limited, due to their short span of existence. Their leader, however, was known to be a man named Ikia Imura. B.J. recognized the fax photo of the man he had held in a choke hold that morning. Only two other members of the gang had been positively identified. Both were women and reported to be sisters. B.J. also recognized these two photos as the two women who had held the hostages at gunpoint and who had become so visibly upset when B.J. had placed the gun against Imura's head. They were not only terrorists, but Imura's mistresses, as well. The only intell on the Cuban participants was so limited that it was virtually useless, but everyone knew they were out there. One was resting in the morgue, and B.J. had met another one, up close and personal.

Erin Hatch entered the room. He was carrying the latest satellite images of the target area. Spreading them out on a table, Johnson and the others gathered around to analyze them. Hatch leaned over the table and tapped his finger on an area directly in the center of the grid that Fisal had designated as the boundaries of the battlefield.

"Here are you hostages," said Hatch. "As you can see, the mangroves and the cypress trees are so thick around the area that a positive body count can't be made by visual sighting."

Pulling a red-spotted, transparent overlay from a cylinder on the table, Hatch placed it over the photos. Red images covered the body shapes that had been visible in the pictures.

"Infrared heat sensor shots from the satellite didn't come out as well as we had hoped. NASA says this is usually for daytime attempts, but that they'll get us a clearer set about midnight tonight. You'll notice the large static heat readings located to the southeast and north of the hostage position. Those are hot springs coming up from underground."

As Hatch explained that phenomenon, Jake silently began counting the body-heat images that were clearly visible within the confines of the holding area. Hatch saw the concern in the man's face as he completed the count. "What's the matter, Jake?" asked Hatch.

"I count only twenty images inside the wire, Erin. They took twenty-five people with them."

Hatch studied the overlay and came up with the same count. In an attempt to halt the growing anxiety of those around the table, Hatch calmly explained, "That's understandable, Jake. Like I said, daytime images are not as accurate as those taken in the cool of the night. The five missing people could be there, but near another heat source which gives the impression there is only one object. We'll get a better count tonight." Pausing, Hatch ran his finger over the images projected around the stockade as he said, "Now, you see all of these—those are the bad guys. I figure close to forty, maybe a few more. This area to the left of the moat is terrorist headquarters."

Lifting the transparent sheet from the photos, he pointed out the empty crates and the freshly dug dirt scattered intermittently around the hostages. "I guess we all know what this is," said Hatch.

"The explosives Fisal talked about on the tape," replied Smith, in a low, pained tone.

"Exactly," said Hatch, "it would appear they are using C-4 plastic—and lots of it."

Will Hayes came into the room. He was carrying a long gun case with him. Moving to the table, he said, "Jonathan, you know the president is on television addressing the nation right now."

Johnson nodded, "Yes, Will, we know. Clinton Bowers called a half hour before the broadcast and gave us an abbreviated version of the speech."

Setting the gun case aside, the CIA director bent over the table and studied the photos. "These the latest ones from overhead?" he asked.

"Yeah," said B.J. "We were hoping to get a fix on some of those damn sensors, but it's too thick through there for a clear view."

Hayes studied the pictures for a few more seconds, then, with an air of refined cockiness and coolness, pointed to the southeast quadrant and said, "That's your way in, gentlemen. The sensors in that area are malfunctioning. They can't get accurate readings from them, and they have no replacements."

Everyone at the table straightened up. Stunned, and with their mouths hanging open, they stared in disbelief at Hayes, who calmly pulled a cigar from his inside coat pocket, lit it, and puffed vigorously, anticipating the inevitable question. His agency had been insulted earlier. Now, he would extract a small degree of pleasure by forcing them to ask that question.

The general realized what the man was doing. It seemed only fitting that since he was the one who had ruffled Hayes's feathers, he should be the one to humble himself in the man's eyes. "William, would you care to enlighten our little group as to how you came by that information?"

Blowing a stream of smoke toward the ceiling, a smiling Hayes said, "I thought you'd never ask, Jonathan. Contrary to what a few people think, we at the agency do land on our feet occasionally." Pulling two cassette tapes from his pocket, he recovered a cassette player from a nearby desk and placed it on the table. Placing a tape in the slot, he set the counter to zero, then fast-forwarded the tape to the numbers he was looking for. Stopping the tape, he looked over at B.J. and said, "Major Mattson, it was fortunate for us that you were in the right place at the right time to receive that tape this morning."

Mattson appeared as confused as the others. "Excuse me, sir, but I'm afraid I don't follow you. The terrorist had hundreds of those tapes distributed all over the country. I just happened to get one of them."

Hayes was grinning as he said, "Ah, but you see, Major, therein lies the difference. All of the other tapes are not the same as the one you received. True, it contains the same bullshit speech by our boy, Fisal—word for word, for that matter. But you see, the others were recorded before Fisal arrived here. Your copy was recorded only a few days ago."

"Now, wait a minute, Will," said Johnson. "I know I pissed you off this afternoon, and now you've got a chance to do a little grandstanding, but just how the hell do you know that?"

With his finger poised over the play button, Hayes replied, "This is a copy of the tape received by CNN News at nine o'clock this morning. It is exactly like those received by the other networks. Now, listen." There was silence as Hayes pressed the button. Fisal's voice was the only sound in the room.

"They illegally infiltrate countries, conduct kidnappings, commit assassinations, and, like pirates, openly fire on ships on the open seas—all in the name of national security. I would ask you, which is the terrorist, and which the freedom fighter?

"For too long now, the Jew-loving—"

Hayes stopped the tape. The men around him glanced at one another, then back to the director. "So what?" said Smith. "We all heard that in the conference room a few hours ago."

"No, Sergeant Smith," said Hayes, replacing the first tape with a second and fast-forwarding it to the position he wanted. "This is what you heard this afternoon." Hayes hit the play button again.

"They illegally infiltrate countries, conduct kidnappings, commit assassinations, and, like pirates, openly fire on ships on the open seas—all in the name of national security. I would ask you, which is the terrorist, and which the freedom fighter?"

There was a slight pause in the tape. In the background, barely audible, was a muffled sound of someone talking. It only lasted a few seconds, then Fisal continued, "For too long now, the Jew-loving politicians—"

Again, Hayes stopped the tape. Looking up at the faces around him, he waited. Impatient, he finally said, "Oh, come now, gentlemen. If an old man of my years can hear it, I'm certain you should be able to."

"Damn, play that again, William," said Johnson.

Hayes rewound the tape and played it again.

"There's a pause in this tape that isn't in the other one," said B.J., "and some kind of background sound—like someone talking."

"Exactly, Major. Very good," said Hayes. "That pause and that sound are not on any of the other tapes that were delivered this morning."

Johnson flashed a look of admiration at Hayes as he asked, "When did you become aware of this, Will?"

"At the meeting this afternoon. I had listened to that broadcast over thirty times by the time we got here. When you played the tape the major had given you, that background noise set off some alert bells in the ol' memory banks. You all looked pretty down at the time; I didn't want to raise any false hopes. It might have been nothing. So, when you all left the room, I pulled the tape and compared it with the ones from this morning. Major Mattson's was different."

"Okay," said Jake, "so how do you know this one was recorded here?"

Hayes was enjoying his moment in the spotlight. His grin widened, "Quite simple, Commander. While I was awaiting the arrival of our special weapon, I took the tape to some friends of ours over at Sony. They washed out the speech, threw in a little high technology, and brought up the background sounds."

Advancing the tape farther, Hayes again hit the play button. Fisal's voice was gone, replaced now by that of a woman with a gravelly voice. She was speaking in German.

As the men around the table listened to the tape, Hayes reached down and picked up the pile of terrorist photos. Searching through them, he set two aside. Another voice, a man's this time, answered the woman in German. There was irritation in his voice. The conversation lasted less than thirty seconds, then Fisal's voice reappeared on the tape. Hayes stopped the recorder.

Raising a questioning eyebrow, General Johnson looked around the room at his men and asked, "Anybody happen to speak German?" No one replied. "Well, then, get me someone that—" Seeing another smile inching its way across the CIA man's face, the general said, "Never mind—okay, Will, go ahead. You speak German, right? And you're going to tell us what they said."

"Better than that, Jonathan. I've even got pictures. A show-and-tell lesson, you might say." Holding up the photos of Eva Schmidt and Kurt Mueller, he continued. "These are the two people you just heard on the tape. Miss Schmidt, here, was complaining to Herr Mueller about a problem with the sensors in the southeast quadrant. It seems they have a malfunction. They project images that are not there, and there are no replacements. Herr Mueller rather rudely informed her that he and his men had been out there on three occasions to repair them. They were not going out again. If they still didn't work, then the hell with them. Seems he doesn't believe you boys will come in from that direction, anyway. End of story."

Jake nodded and said, "I see your point now, Mr. Hayes. Those sensors were not put into position until Fisal arrived in Florida. Therefore, the tape could only have been made a few days ago—here."

"I knew I could count on a Harvard man," laughed Hayes.

General Johnson reached across the table and shook the

man's hand firmly as he said, "William, I take back every bad thing I have ever said about you and your super spooks. You did a fine job on this thing."

"That's quite all right, Jonathan, but you're the ones who are going to have to do the nasty work. Have you figured out who is going on this little expedition with you?"

"Not yet. We've been too busy trying to figure a way in there without getting our asses shot off in the first ten minutes," said Tommy Smith.

"Well, it would seem that problem has been solved, thanks to Mr. Hayes," said B.J. "Now would be as good a time as any to do a team breakdown, General."

The general agreed. "All right, then. We know that Major Mattson, Commander Mortimer, and I are three of the required players. Sergeant Smith, it goes without saying that you are the fourth. I am going to put you with B.J., if that is acceptable to you."

"Airborne, sir!" replied the stocky sergeant.

"That just leaves you and me without a dance partner, Jake. Any suggestions?" asked Johnson.

"I'm afraid that just leaves you, sir," said Jake. "As soon as I heard Fisal's plan, I took it upon myself to contact a friend of mine. We do a lot of hunting together and something like this would be right up his alley. He should be here soon. The guards at the gate are going to let me know when he arrives."

Mattson lit a cigarette as he asked, "Is this friend of yours a SEAL, Ranger, or Green Beret?"

"None of the above, B.J.—he's a civilian."

"What!" said Johnson and Hayes in unison. "A civilian?" cried Hayes. "My Lord, son, these are hard-core terrorists you're going after out there, not some deer you can take a potshot at from a blind."

"Easy, gentlemen, the man is a Vietnam vet, force

Marine recon, sniper, and tracker. Name's Johnny Okiela-lee. He's a full-blooded Seminole, born and raised in the Big Cypress area. The man's got night vision like a cat's and he's about as tough as they come." Turning to Hayes, Jake continued, "And it's not deer, Mr. Hayes. It's alligators. We don't kill them. I help him catch them for zoos across the country."

Johnson laughed as he said, "No one can say we don't have a diversified group in SOCOM. Who would believe an alligator-wrestling SEAL with a Harvard law degree? You know, Mr. Mortimer, you just might make a name for yourself in this outfit—if you survive long enough."

Everyone laughed, then Smith said, "Well, sir, that just leaves one more selection, and it's your call. Any ideas, sir?"

Johnson hooked a leg over the corner of the table and thought for a moment. Finding volunteers for this mission was not a problem. Since the attack, SOCOM had received a multitude of calls from nearly every military unit in the country. All were willing to take on Fisal and his terrorists.

Erin Hatch moved his hulking six-four frame through the group and stepped in front of Johnson. Snapping to attention, he saluted and barked, "Sir, I would consider it both an honor and a privilege to accompany the general on this little ass-kicking convention."

Johnson rose to his feet and returned the salute of his senior intelligence officer. "You have a wife and children, Major Hatch. You may want to reconsider that request."

Hatch's steel-blue eyes never wavered as he replied, "A lot of people had wives and kids until this morning, sir. My wife, Mary Ellen, is a hell of an army wife, sir. We had a lot of friends hurt, or worse, out there today. She'd be disappointed if I didn't go. We both believe in the payback theory, sir. It would be an honor for both of us if you would allow me to tag along, sir."

"Hear, hear!" came the cheer from the group around the table. Johnson placed his hand on Hatch's broad shoulders. "Looks like you got yourself a job, son."

"Thank you, sir," said Hatch with pride as B.J. and the others slapped him on the back.

The pleasantry of the moment ended abruptly as the communications officer burst into the room. "Sir! You better come quick. Fisal's on the radio and he's mad as hell! Says there are thirty armed men moving into his A.O. He thinks we're dealing off the bottom of the deck, sir. Says he's going to kill the hostages—wants to talk to you."

"Shit!" yelled B.J. "I was afraid of this. Somebody sat around drinking and talked themselves into believing they're all fuckin' Rambos."

"Better hurry, sir," said the commo officer, "the guy sounded serious about the hostages."

A wave of men streamed down the hall behind the general. The sergeant at the communications console stood and backed away from the radio mike. "He's pretty pissed, sir. Thinks we broke the rules before the game even started."

Johnson sat down behind the mike. The room was silent. "Fisal, this is General J. J. Johnson, SOCOM commander. We have no idea what you are talking about. I have just this minute made the selections of the three men who will play your little game in the morning. Do you hear me, Fisal? We have no people out there tonight. That area is supposed to be off limits to everyone but us. Do you copy, Fisal?"

Haunting seconds of silence seemed like hours before Fisal replied. Johnson could sense the strain in the man's voice as he struggled to maintain his composure. "If not your people, General, who?"

Johnson's eyes immediately shot toward Hayes. The CIA man raised his hands and waved them in front of him, vigorously shaking his head from side to side as he said, "No way, Jonathan—they're not ours."

"I'm waiting, General!" said Fisal, impatiently.

"Listen, Fisal. I have no way of knowing who those people are. It could be a group of irate citizens. You killed a lot of civilians today; then you told the world where you were going to be. What did you expect? I can only give you my word that none of those people are in any way connected to the government or the military." Johnson paused to think, then said, "Fisal, I'm certain a man who has planned as carefully as you have for this day must have night vision capabilities within your arsenal. Have your people identify the types of weapons these intruders are carrying. If I am correct, they will find a mishmash of hunting rifles and shotguns. Hardly the type of equipment a paramilitary force moving on the offensive would carry. That should prove to you that neither I nor any other agency has broken the rules of your game. Will you do that?"

Fisal's words were icy. "I warned you, General. Any violation of my rules and the hostages would die. No second chances. Remember?"

"Jesus Christ, man! We've done everything humanly possible to keep this thing under control and comply with your demands. At least verify what I've said before you act. That is the least you can do."

Across the room, Sergeant Smith whispered, "Oh, God, please."

B. J. Mattson's stomach tightened into a painful knot as he tried to remember the last words he had spoken to his wife and kids.

Fisal purposely hesitated in giving a response. Fear was indeed a powerful weapon. "Very well, General. I will do as you suggest, then I will decide the fate of the prisoners. I shall contact you again shortly." There was a click and the radio went silent. Johnson locked his fingers, raised his hands, and leaned his head on them. His thoughts were of Helen.

No one moved. No one spoke. It was as if the room had been suspended in time. Five minutes passed and the anxious men could do nothing but wait.

"General Johnson." The sudden words startled those in the room. It was Fisal. "General, are you still there?"

"Yes, I am here. Your results, sir?"

Fisal's tone seemed calmer now. "Your suspicions were correct, General. It is obvious by their weapons and the drunken, undisciplined manner in which they are stumbling around in the dark that these people are not military in any sense of the word. They are simply more ignorant Americans who overestimate their own power."

"The hostages, Fisal. What is your decision?" asked Johnson.

Again, Fisal purposely waited before giving his reply. "They shall be spared, General, but be warned a final time. Any more such incidents as this one, and I will not bother to contact you again. We will simply destroy the hostages and the camp, then fade away into the swamps. There will be no second chances, General, do you understand?"

"Yes—I—I understand."

"In order that others might be discouraged from attempting such foolishness, I shall personally make an example of these fools who dared enter here," said Fisal, sadistically.

"What do you intend to do, Fisal?"

"You shall see, General. In the morning, you, your press, the world for that matter, shall see what fate awaits those who violate the rules of Allah's game. It is good that you are a man of your word, General Johnson. That is honorable. I shall look forward to meeting you on the field of battle tomorrow. Until then, farewell."

The radio went silent again. Johnson slumped back in his chair. The tension of the last few minutes had drained him.

A sergeant peeked in the door. Spotting Jake, he moved to his side and whispered, "Sir, the guards at the gate just called. They've got an Indian down there who says he's supposed to see you. Quite a sight, from what they say. Big fellow—Indian dress, bow and arrows, and a damn CAR-15 assault rifle on a string hanging round his neck. You know this guy, Commander?"

Jake laughed quietly to himself. That was Johnny. He always came prepared. "Yes, Sergeant, I sure do. Tell them I'll be right down to pick him up."

"Yes, sir," said the sergeant, who turned and left the room to comply with the order as General Johnson leaned his head back and stared up at the ceiling. There was pity in his voice as he said, "Those poor, drunken bastards. They're one step from hell's gate, and don't even know it."

Marcus Taylor placed two men on point. They had been in the swamps for over two hours, but it seemed much longer. Murky, moss-covered water grabbed at their knees as they struggled to maintain their footing in mud and tangled undergrowth. Noise discipline was nonexistent. The same was true of light discipline. Glowing cigarettes and flashlights could be seen all along the line of Taylor's army. The beams from unstable flashlights shone on the water, in the treetops, and occasionally along the banks.

Red Culder moved up next to Marcus. "Ya know, maybe this ain't such a good idea after all, Marcus. I mean, man, we're sure makin' a lot of noise out here. Don't you think so?"

Taylor stopped. Cradling his twelve gauge shotgun, he pulled a pint of whiskey from his back pocket. Unscrewing the cap, he downed a long swallow, then passed the bottle to Culder. "Have a drink, Red. You just let me take care of the military business out here, okay? I'm the expert, remember."

Culder took the bottle and stared at the half-drunken leader of this expedition. Red had an uncomfortable gut feeling that maybe—just maybe—Marcus Taylor wasn't the big jungle expert everyone thought he was. The doubt began when Red watched one of the boys toss an empty liquor bottle into some mangrove trees about an hour ago. In the past hour, Red had spotted that same bottle twice. He was pretty well lit, but hell, even he could tell they were going around in circles. He started to say something about that to Taylor, but he let it go. Taylor could be a belligerent son of a bitch when he was drinking, and this wasn't the time or the place for a knock-down, drag-out fistfight. Tipping the bottle back a second time, Red took a healthy drink and passed it back to Marcus. "Sure, Marcus, you're the expert."

Somewhere behind them, there was a splash, as one of the men tripped and fell face first into the water. Pulling himself up, he wiped the soggy moss from his face and neck. "Fuck this shit," he said. "Hell, what are we doin'? Let's make them bastards come to us!" Raising his 30.06 deer rifle, he fired three rapid shots into the air.

The ear-shattering blasts set off a panic among the men of Taylor's private army. Suddenly, everyone was shooting in all directions. In a matter of seconds, they were engaged in a full-fledged firefight with themselves. A man screamed out in pain as double-odd buckshot ricocheted off the trunk of a rock-hard cypress tree and tore through the man's right shoulder. "They got Charlie! They done shot Charlie!" yelled someone. The firing increased. Another man groaned as a rifle slug tore through his left leg. The man who had shot was trying to reload his rifle. Culder looked to Taylor for guidance. The great jungle fighter was hiding behind the base of mangrove trees, shaking like a leaf, and trying to force a shotgun shell into his weapon backward.

Culder waded toward Taylor. Reaching down, he grabbed the shotgun from the man. "Some damn war hero you turned out to be! Give me that before you fuckin' hurt somebody." Turning his back on Taylor, Red moved out into the center of the water and began yelling, "Stop firing! Stop firing, god damn it! There ain't nobody out there. You're shootin' the hell out of each other! Stop firing!"

Slowly the firing subsided. Culder was in control at last. "Some of you boys help Fred and Murphy over there. Try to stop that bleedin'. Rest of you, get on back here. We're gettin' the fuck outta this place before we get ourselves in any more trouble."

A series of shots rang out from up near the point position. Culder turned in time to see the muzzle flashes from a gun barrel. "God damn it!" growled Culder as he tossed Taylor's empty shotgun back to him and began sloshing his way in the direction of the shooting. "I done told you boys to knock that shit off. We're gettin' outta here, an' I don't want no more shootin'." No one answered.

Pulling a flashlight from his pocket, Red shone its light ahead of him as he moved forward. "Hey, Reggie! You boys hear what I said? I—" Culder stopped suddenly as the glow of the light came to rest on the back of a body floating facedown in the water. White down feathers soaked in blood protruded from the four exit holes in the back of the cream-colored hunting jacket Reggie was wearing. Reluctantly inching himself forward, Red Culder reached out and slowly rolled the body over in the water. "Jesus!" he cried, as he jerked his hand back. Half of Reggie's face was missing.

"Even Jesus can't help you now, fool."

Culder swung the light toward the bank. His mouth dropped open as the light fell on the three forms standing less than ten yards from him. For a mere bartender, the sight of men dressed in full combat gear with hand grenades hanging from their web gear was indeed a startling revelation. Fisal, Mueller, and Imura were all grinning. Their automatic weapons were leveled at Culder. Red knew he was a dead man.

Taylor was coming up to see what the problem was. "Hey, Red, you can't just take over, you know. I mean this is my fuckin' little army out here. I say when we leave. You hear me?"

Mueller winked at Culder. Tilting his rifle up slightly, he whispered, "Bye-bye, Red."

The shot hit Culder square in the mouth, blowing the back of his head out. Taylor flinched at the sound of the shot and brought up his flashlight. At the same instant, part of Red's brain splattered the front of his shirt. Culder's body stiffened for a second, then dropped like a giant redwood.

"Oh, God!" screamed Taylor. Throwing his shotgun down, he raised his hands. "Don't shoot! Please don't shoot! I didn't want no part of this. They made me come out here. I ain't got nothin' against you guys. Please—please."

Fisal removed the cap from the long, silver, star cluster in his hand. Holding it out in front of him, he slammed the base of the metal against his palm. The flare shot out like a skyrocket, climbing into the night sky. Taylor's army turned their heads upward and watched as the streaking light reached its peak, then burst into a brilliant white glare. The small parachute oscillated slowly back and forth as it floated back to earth. "Man, that's some neat shit," said one of the civilians. They hadn't bothered to watch the bank.

The terrorists waiting there watched for Fisal's signal. When it came, they all fired at the same time. Bullets ripped through the mob of hapless men who had clustered together in a tight circle. The roar of gunfire was deafening as hot lead blew heads apart, tore gaping holes through their chests, legs, and arms. The bullets were hitting the water around the screaming, dying men like heavy raindrops. Taylor threw his hands up to his ears, trying desperately to shout out the cries of his dying friends.

Finally, mercifully, it was over. The swamp fell silent again. A heavy gray cloud of gunsmoke drifted slowly over the moss-covered water, which had become a carpet of blood. The thick, red color washed up against the twisting, turning branches of the trees, leaving its mark on the trunks as the floating pile of bodies bobbed slowly up and down and drifted toward Taylor.

Mueller placed a fresh magazine in his rifle, let the bolt go forward, and sighted in on Taylor's forehead. Fisal reached out and pushed the barrel down. "No, this one wished to be their leader. So he shall be. Like the bad shepherd, he has led his sheep to the slaughter. For this, he deserves honor among his flock. It is only fitting that we provide him that honor."

The echoing sounds of gunfire carried on the night air. General Sweet, who had decided to remain with the women, for their protection, of course, sat straight up. "Wha—what is that?" he asked, still half-asleep.

"Sounds like a firefight, General," said Jason Mattson.

"Yeah," said Troy Smith, "and a one-sided one, at that. Those are AK-47s firing automatic."

"Damn it!" gasped Sweet. "I should have known Johnson and those idiots of his would screw this up. The terrorists will kill us for sure, now."

Nancy Smith sat up, glared at Sweet, and said, "Oh, why don't you shut up, Sweet! You don't know what the hell you're talking about."

The little general was taken aback by the sudden rebuke. "I beg your pardon, madam. I'll have you know I had my own command in Vietnam, and believe me, I caused more than my share of trouble for those little Vietnamese bastards in that war."

"Yes, I'm sure you did, General," said Nancy cuttingly, "but for which side? North or South? We know all about you, General Sweet. How you got your position in SO-COM, and why you are there. Well, it's a little different this time, isn't it? This time it's your butt that's on the line, and the only people who can save that fat ass of yours are the same men whose careers you've been trying to destroy for the last two years. Rather ironic, don't you think so?"

Sweet's cheeks were puffing in and out with rage. He was a general. He did not have to take abuse from a mere woman.

"Now, see here, lady. Such irresponsible accusations are no more than hearsay. No one can prove I have done anything to jeopardize SOCOM's assigned missions—no one."

Charlotte Mattson was awakened by the heated exchange and sat up as Sweet said, "The organization itself is functional, it is the leadership that is incompetent and undisciplined. General Johnson, with his buddy-buddy attitude toward his men, is highly irregular and totally unacceptable for a man of his position. A commander must be firm, demanding, and unwavering, not some kindly old grandfather with white hair who pats them on the head every time they manage to do something right."

Raymond Sweet was fired up and on a roll, now. "Just look at the two men he calls his top troubleshooters—a hotshot, rich boy from Boston who spends half his time chasing women and the other half causing nothing but trouble in the community, and then there's that over-the-hill major who can't even keep his own marriage together. No, young woman, you have it all wrong. I am merely trying to restore some sense of order within that command, not destroy it."

"What a crock!" said Troy Smith.

"Amen!" replied the boy's mother, who turned to see that Charlotte was awake and had surely heard Sweet's remarks about their marriage. Patting Charlotte softly on the leg, she said, "Don't pay any attention to this ol' windbag, honey; he doesn't know what he's talking about."

Sweet's face turned crimson. Pulling a pen and piece of paper from his shirt pocket, he snapped, "All right, that's it. I've had enough of this disgraceful conduct from you, lady. We might just get out of this thing somehow, and if we do, I want to remember you. Your husband must work at the base. What's his name, and where does he work? I want to have a personal talk with him when we get out of here."

Troy Smith didn't care for the tone of Sweet's voice.

Nancy saw the aggression building in the boy's eyes and stopped him before he grabbed the little general. "My name is Nancy Smith. My husband is Master Sergeant Tommy Smith, senior crew chief of the Special Operations Wing of SOCOM—the same crew chief you almost got killed in Ecuador two years ago with your damn interference."

Sweet was writing furiously as he said, "Well, you can bet that if I do get out of this, he may wish he had stayed in

Ecuador. Him, that damn Major Mattson, and Jake Mortimer, too."

"It's Colonel! Colonel Mattson," said Charlotte softly.

"What?" asked Sweet, looking up at the attractive blond.

"It's Colonel B. J. Mattson, General, not major. The
rank was official as of midnight last night."

"And just who might you be? His latest girlfriend?"
snickered Sweet.

Jason Mattson was on the man before anyone could react.
Grabbing the front of the general's shirt, his fists twisted the
collar tightly, as he slammed Sweet back on the ground.
"Listen, asshole, my father would never do anything to hurt
our mother, especially shit like that." Tightening his grip,
the boy leaned closer to Sweet's face. "You know, man,
you really got an attitude problem. I mean—"

"Jason! Let that man go at once! Do you hear me?"

Jason looked back at his mother. Her voice was stern, but
there was a gleam of pride in her eyes. "Do it now, son."

The boy released his grip and backed away.

"Troy, why don't you and Jason go check on your sisters
and the other children. Okay?" said Nancy.

"Sure, Mom. Come on, Jason."

The two boys stood and walked away. Sweet pulled
himself back up to a sitting position, rubbed at his neck and
then began smoothing out the front of his wrinkled shirt.

"I am sorry, General Sweet. I'm afraid my son has his
father's temper," said Charlotte.

"You should be sorry, madam. Just who is his father?"

Nancy shook her head sadly as she said, "You see,
General, that is the difference between you and General
Johnson. He makes a point of knowing everything and
everyone in his command, even their families. This is
Charlotte Mattson, B.J.'s wife, not his girlfriend, and that
boy who wanted to take your head off is their son. Their

daughter, Angela, is here, too, General. Just as Tommy Smith's entire family is here, so is B.J.'s. Do you understand what I'm saying, General Sweet? If you degrade our husbands in front of their children, then you must expect a reaction."

Sweet lowered his head and stared blankly at the piece of paper he still clutched in his hand.

"Do you really dislike my husband so, General?" asked Charlotte.

Sweet did not answer, nor did he look at the woman.

"Oh, it's quite all right, General. There was a time, not long ago, that I, too, had a great dislike for the man. I thought my life and that of our children would be better off without him. You see, General, he was obsessed with his work—even when I took his children and deserted him, he continued on with his job. I never understood why, not until now. I see the hatred in the faces of these men who murder in the name of their god; I look into the frightened eyes of the women and children here, and then I understand."

"Wha—what do you understand, Mrs. Mattson?" asked Sweet humbly, without looking up.

"I understand that B.J. and men like him are all that stand between the dictators, drug dealers, and terrorists like these and the innocent people of the world. They give them hope. B.J. and the others risk their lives every time the innocent are in trouble, even for you, General Sweet. B.J. never talked about his work, but then, I never asked. He knew I hated this military life. How hard it must have been for him, wanting to reach out when the nightmares would come, but knowing I wouldn't understand. No, General, it was not Colonel Mattson who couldn't keep his marriage together, it was his wife's lack of understanding. I can promise you, General Sweet, if we survive this, you will never have cause to say anything like that again. As I said, I'm sorry, and I apologize for my son's actions, but he is very close to his father. I hope you understand."

Sweet crumpled the piece of paper in his hand and dropped it and the pen on the ground. Nodding, he silently stood and quietly walked away.

Helen Cantrell came over to where Nancy and Charlotte were and sat down. She had spent the last few hours with Beverly Mills. Fisal had kept the reporter in his quarters for over three hours. When they returned her to the stockade, her clothes were bloodstained and torn and she was in a state of severe shock. The women had tried to make her as comfortable as possible. There was little else they could do. Nancy asked how she was doing.

Helen Cantrell folded her hands in her lap and leaned back to stare up through an opening in the trees at the stars above. "That poor girl. It may be years before she is over the trauma of what happened this evening. When she tries to speak, her whole body begins to shake, and she bursts into tears. She keeps trying to say something about that blond woman—the German woman who was with Fisal. When I ask her what she means, she turns pale and curls up in a little ball. It's just terrible. I finally got her to sleep, the poor dear. Hopefully, the rest will do her good, and she will be better in the morning.

"Did General Sweet have any idea what that shooting was about?"

"No," said Nancy. "All he could do was criticize General Johnson and preach of impending doom. You know how he is."

"Oh, yes," answered Helen, her voice sounding tired, "but J.J. and the others will come, and it will be soon. We have only to wait."

The women talked for a few minutes; then Helen rose to go check on Beverly Mills again. She asked if they would like to go with her. Nancy said she would go, but Charlotte declined.

"We won't be long, Charlotte," said Nancy. "You should try to go back to sleep."

Charlotte nodded that she would try, as she watched the two women make their way across the compound. Seeing the crumpled piece of paper Sweet had dropped, she picked it and the pen up before moving closer to one of the lights hanging from the wire. Making herself comfortable, she thought of B.J. as she began to write. Suddenly, it seemed there was so much to tell her husband and so little time.

CHAPTER *11*

Day 5—0400 hours
Helicopter Pad
MacDill AFB

The men of the SOCOM team stood in full combat gear, silently watching the pilots perform the preflight checks on the Blackhawk helicopter that would fly them to the Big Cypress Swamp. Less than fifty yards away, a second chopper was going through the same ritual. Another six-man team stood by, waiting to board that helicopter. It was all part of an elaborate plan designed to give Johnson and his team an edge against the superior numbers under Fisal's command. It would be a limited stalling tactic, but it might provide enough time for the real team to close in on the hostages' position.

The planning portion of the operation did not begin until after Jake had introduced his friend, Johnny Okielalee, to the other members of the team. The big Indian's pleasing smile and personable attitude won the team over almost immediately. Johnny stood six foot four, with wide shoulders and a powerful-looking chest. His hair was pulled back in a ponytail. His light blue eyes, a highly unusual color for an Indian, stood out in his darkly tanned face. There was little doubt that the man was in excellent condition and more than capable of dealing with the situation.

Within minutes of being shown the battle area, Johnny was drawing trails and canal cutaway routes that were not projected by the satellite photos. Many of them the forest rangers did not even know existed. The Indian's knowledge of the area became invaluable. It was easy, now, to see why Mueller had not been overly concerned about the defective sensors in the southeastern quadrant. It was not only the thickest part of the target area, but the most dangerous. Sump holes and water drop-offs were everywhere. It was also the area most heavily populated by alligators and every kind of snake prevalent to the Florida swamps. Throw in an excessive amount of quicksand and acres of dense mangrove trees with twisting, tangling vines, and you had a formidable and challenging walk ahead of you.

Johnny estimated that by taking limited breaks along the way, they could cover the distance to the terrorist base camp in twelve hours, or in eighteen hours if they wanted to move at a more moderate pace. From the look in the eyes of the men who were standing around him, Johnny Okielalee doubted there would be anything moderate about this trip.

Two key elements provided the basis for the operations plan. One, the defective sensors, provided a way in. The other, the ill-fated intrusion into the area by armed civilians, gave justification for stalling for time. SOCOM planned to use both of these factors to their advantage.

At 0430 hours, Johnson and his team would board the first chopper, swing wide around to the southeast, and be inserted one mile from the boundary line of Fisal's battle area. From here, they would move straight into the swamp and toward the base camp, quietly taking out any terrorists they encountered along the way. At 0600 hours, chopper two would lift off and carry the other team around to the west and set them down between the highway and the swamp. The Florida Highway Patrol reported that the highway was already swarming with news crews, cameras, and communications vans from around the world. The arrival of the chopper was sure to cause enough commotion to keep the terrorists' attention focused on the activities to the west.

Fisal had provided a radio frequency that would give the team direct access to him and his headquarters. Once the Americans were ready to begin the game, they had only to notify him by radio. Johnson planned to withhold that signal as long as possible. The decoy helicopter and team would arrive on site at 0630 hours. They would stall for another two hours, or until Fisal called them, asking about the delay. When that call came, and they knew it would, they would inform the terrorist leader that a rumor of another planned civilian raid into the area had been reported and that they were taking actions to eliminate the planned intrusion, but that it would take time. They wanted no mistakes before they began the game. This should provide them with another couple of hours before Fisal would become impatient and call a second time. By then, Johnson and his team would be halfway to the base camp. When that ruse began to wear thin, they always had the press. At just the right time, Will Hayes would leak the radio frequency to a few reporters in the crowd. If they were right, Fisal could not resist the chance to voice his holy cause on worldwide news. That, and a flood of questions coming constantly over his radio should keep him tied up for another hour or two. After that, Hayes and the other team would have to come up with something on their own—anything short of allowing that team to enter the swamp. It was a long shot, at best, that they could pull it off. If there was gunfire before they reached the camp, Fisal would know he had been tricked, and the hostages would die.

From 1000 feet, B.J. stared out across the vastness of the Florida Everglades. It seemed endless. Along the horizon the telltale line of approaching gray signaled the coming of dawn. By the time this day came to an end, a lot of people were going to die. Mattson studied the faces of the men who were about to venture into hell with him. Johnny had traded his bow and arrow for a crossbow, preferring the needle pointed steel bolts to the feathered arrows. Relaxing against his seat, the Indian shifted the shoulder holster that contained a 9mm Beretta, a side arm that each man on the team carried. An MP5 submachine lay on the floor beside him. If the man was concerned about the operation, he wasn't showing it. His eyes were closed and his head rested against the seat.

Erin Hatch sat beside Johnny. He saw B.J. looking his way and smiled a nervous smile. It had been a lot of years since Hatch had been in on a hot operation, but there were just some things a Vietnam vet never forgot. Knowing when to be scared was one of them. Next to Hatch, sat General Johnson. Ol' Q-Tip appeared as cool as a cucumber. Adjusting his web gear, checking his shoulder holster, glancing at his watch every now and then—all repetitive things that a combat soldier did from habit when preparing for battle.

Jake and Tommy sat across from B.J. Jake was staring out the small window at the shimmering water below. His thoughts were of Beverly Mills and the last intimate moments they had spent together in her hotel room the night before this nightmare had begun. He could still feel the smoothness of her back and hear the soft moans she made in his ear when they had made slow, passionate love. She was the first woman in a long time who had made him feel that maybe, just maybe, it was time to settle down.

Tommy bent down and secured the gun case that held the cannon so affectionately referred to as Big Dick. He had talked Jake into letting him carry the big gun. Visions of loading the giant weapon, placing the barrel against Fisal's forehead, and pulling the trigger, danced through Tommy's mind. If they had hurt any member of his family, that was exactly what he was going to do to every last one of the bastards. Sitting back in his seat, he winked at B.J. and gave the thumbs-up sign. B.J. returned the sign and sat back in his seat. They were as ready as they ever would be, and the LZ was coming up fast.

"Two minutes, General!" yelled the crew chief through cupped hands. Johnson nodded, then flashed the time to the others, who began positioning themselves in their seats for the exit from the chopper. The crew chief threw the doors open. Warm air rushed in, swirling about among the anxious men. The Blackhawk banked hard right, then swooped down in a rapid decline, pulling up thirty yards off the ground, hovering, it lowered itself toward the ground. Johnson didn't wait for the skids to touch down. He was out the door at twenty feet, hit the ground, rolled, and took a position in the tall grass. The remaining members of the team were right behind him. In less than ten seconds the chopper had dropped its load and was climbing for altitude, on its way out of the area.

The team lay perfectly still for a full minute. The night surrounded them. Slowly, the sounds of the swamp's natural inhabitants, frightened by the roar of the chopper, began to give voice once again. Birds chirped or whistled and frogs croaked. Somewhere in the distance, a Florida panther growled its displeasure at having been awakened from its sleep.

Johnson activated the small radio in his shirt pocket and placed the whisper mike over his head, adjusting it only inches from his mouth. The others did the same. The radios were only good for short-distance communications up to one-half mile, but that was all they were going to need for the team commo. B.J. was carrying the long-range radio so they could monitor Fisal's frequency and keep up with the progress of their plan.

The mikes for the team's radios were voice-activated. Speaking in a whisper, Johnson made a communications check with each member of the team. All radios were working. "Johnny," said Johnson, "you and Jake take the point. It's a one-way trip from here on out. Let's do it."

Jake linked up with Johnny, and the two men moved into the trees. Easing themselves silently into the knee-deep water, they began moving northwest. Johnson gave them a two-minute head start, then took the rest of the team forward. As they began to enter the water, Johnson pointed to Hatch, designating him the responsibility for rear security. The intell officer nodded and remained on the bank until Johnson and the others were out of sight. Making one last check of the LZ, Hatch climbed down into the murky water and made his way forward, pausing every now and then to check behind him.

The darkness was beginning to lift as dawn approached. Johnny stopped and whispered to Jake, "We'll make better time as soon as the sun comes up."

"That's good, Johnny," said a nervous Jake Mortimer, his eyes darting back and forth across the dark water.

"What's wrong, Jake?" asked the Indian, sensing his nervousness.

"I don't know, man. Hell, gators don't bother me, but, damn, I hate those fuckin' snakes."

Johnny grinned. "Well, just stay close. I'll keep an eye

out for them. We won't have to stay in this water long. I know where there's a trail about a mile up. We can parallel it most of the way."

"Hell, let's keep moving, then. A mile in this shit can seem like forever."

Johnny quietly moved on. Jake was close behind. He led them through a dream world of gray cypresses, silent Spanish moss, and knee-deep watery sloughs. There was a haunting beauty about the place, threatening, yet peaceful.

Jake stopped suddenly. A speckled, six-foot king snake lay on a small log only a few feet from him. Johnny moved quietly back to Jake and goaded the snake into gliding off into the canal. It swam across the narrow waterway and into a patch of brush. Jake nodded his thanks and moved out behind Johnny as he once again took the point.

B. J. Mattson glanced down into the sparkling water. It was rather like black Costa Rican coffee, he thought as he glided along to catch up with the others. Up ahead, Johnny had stopped to get his bearings. He looked upstream to where the water flowed out of a tunnel in the fringe of moonvines at the edge of the bayhead. Through the tunnel he could see open space back inside under the overhanging trees. The water in there was shaded. Here and there its surface glistened with quick flashes of gold light. Pointing that direction, Johnny waded out from the bank and into waist-deep water. Jake hesitated for a moment, then followed the Seminole as he walked up through the low opening in the vine tangle. Under the arched ceiling of ash, maple, and pond cypress trees only little rays of early morning sunlight came in. They gleamed green-gold and amber on the leaves and glossy water.

Jake could see that if they followed the channel upstream, they would pass from one such vaulted chamber to another, all connected by tunnels through the tangled vines over the deeper runs. The place was cool, almost dreamlike, and different from anywhere Jake had ever been. The scent of ghost orchids in bloom filled the water-floored room like a greenhouse at Easter time.

Johnny waited until Johnson and the others had entered the chamber, then proceeded on to the next.

"This is really something, isn't it?" said Jake as B.J. paused next to him and adjusted the straps of his rucksack.

"Yeah," replied B.J. "Kind of a cross between Vietnam and Disneyland."

They continued on for another hour, moving in and out of the chambers and tunnels, until finally Johnny signaled toward the bank. He had found the trail he had been watching for. It was a welcome relief for the team. They had spent the last two hours in the water, and B.J. was beginning to feel like a prune, all wrinkled and worn out. From somewhere above them, there came an unsettling sort of wailing cry—both wild and strange. Johnny grinned at the startled look the sound elicited from the men as he helped them from the water. "Only the limpkin bird, gentlemen. He likes to scare the hell out of people."

Hatch was the last man to move toward the bank. Reaching up, he grabbed a limb to pull himself out of the water. The limb snapped loudly and broke in his hand, sending the big man splashing backward into the water. A belly-deep roar came from a patch of willows not thirty feet from Hatch. Johnny reached out and grabbed Hatch, pulling him quickly up onto the bank.

"What the hell was that?" asked Hatch in a hurried breath.

Johnny pointed to the cluster of willow switches. The old alligator sloshed into a new position in six inches of water and mud, where it swelled its body and roared once more.

"Shit," said Hatch. "I wasn't bothering the ol' boy."

Johnny smiled. "I know—look."

Hatch and the others watched as twenty or thirty baby alligators swarmed around and over the big gator. "It's a female. She took the sound of the breaking branch and the splash for a neighbor that might be thinking of moving into her nursery."

Hatch laughed as he wiped his hands on his fatigue shirt. "Don't worry, ol' girl, I've got two kids at home. Thirty of 'em running around the house would drive me nuts."

The thought of moving on a trail was totally alien to Mattson. A lesson learned in Vietnam. Johnny knelt down and studied the ground. There were prints of the Florida panther, opossums galore, and a few triangular prints with a tail mark between them, made by armadillos. There were no human prints. Johnny had not expected to find any. Only a few Indians knew of this trail. Looking back at General Johnson, the Seminole could see that the pace at which they were moving was taking its toll on the sixty-year-old commander. Johnny asked if anyone wanted to rest before moving on. Johnson shook his head no. They could rest when it was over.

0830 hours
Southwest Quadrant
Highway 84

Will Hayes stood near the communications van. The radios inside were all set on Fisal's frequency. The highway that formed the Everglades Parkway had been closed. Nearly a thousand people, most of them television and newspaper reporters, formed a line that stretched for miles. The CNN News crew arrived before daylight, not expecting to have anything to report before 8:00 A.M. They had planned to show the charred remains of the helicopters that still smoldered in the field between the highway and the boundary of the swamps where Fisal's game was to begin. When daylight finally came, they discovered they had more to show than a bunch of blown-up, smoldering helicopters.

Fisal's warning to those who would attempt to interfere in this holy battle was made very clear to a shocked public who awoke to discover the terrible face of death staring back at them from their television sets.

The bodies of twenty-nine men hung from the trees just beyond the burned-out helicopters. Their clothes were bloodstained and torn. It was a gruesome sight, but not nearly as frightening as the pitiful sight that stood in front of the burned-out choppers. A makeshift cross had been placed just inside the off-limits area. Marcus Taylor's hands and feet were nailed to the cross. A one-inch-wide piece of wet rawhide was placed around his neck and secured to the cross. He was still alive.

Will Hayes asked Fisal for the man's life. Fisal refused. Anyone who crossed that line, other than the SOCOM team, would cause the death of the hostages. No one could do anything for Marcus Taylor. The cameras zoomed in on the tortured face of the man who had envisioned himself on nationwide television as a hero. Now he had his media attention. But with the rise in temperature as the day progressed, the rawhide would shrink and draw tighter around Taylor's neck. Camera crews pushed and shoved to get into position as they watched the sun and called for temperature readings every few minutes. The entire thing made Hayes sick to his stomach. If he had his way, he would run the whole damn bunch out of here; but then they'd start screaming about First Amendment rights, the freedom of the press, and all that bullshit. It wasn't worth the hassle. Besides, the longer they kept focused on that poor bastard on the cross, the less attention would be paid to the six-man combat team that waited across the field near the swamp. The newspeople were so entranced by watching a man die that they had not yet asked what was delaying the Americans moving in after Fisal. Surprisingly, neither had Fisal.

Hayes glanced down at his watch. Jonathan and the boys had been on the ground nearly four hours. By now, they would have covered one-third of the distance to the camp. But how long could they stall? Fisal was bound to get impatient soon.

0900 hours
Terrorist Base Camp

Fisal pressed his mike switch and asked for a report from Imura and the Red Team, who were positioned near the edge of the southwest quadrant. They had a clear view of the highway and the six-man team that waited nearby. Imura kept trying to focus his binoculars on the faces of the team, but it did little good. They wore heavy camouflage paint, making positive identification impossible from that distance. Imura reported their arrival at 0630 in the morning, but since then, they had done little but move down from the highway and wait. The little Japanese had no idea what the delay was and informed Fisal that nothing had changed since his report an hour ago.

Fisal tossed the mike aside and walked to the doorway. Staring out at the hostages, who were nervously milling around in the stockade, he sensed that something was wrong, but he wasn't quite sure what it was. It would appear that the Americans were doing as he had asked. They simply were not ready for the game to begin. But, sooner or later they would have to come to him. The timer on the charges placed around the hostages had been set. They had no choice. Time was running out.

Eva Schmidt came out of the radar/electronics hut. She seemed troubled about something. Fisal called to her, and she joined him at the doorway. "What is it, Ms. Schmidt? You look worried."

Eva didn't care much for Fisal, but she had to admit he was an effective leader. "Oh, it's nothing, really. I only wish Kurt was here."

"You know he and his team are already in position behind Mr. Imura. We cannot move them now. What is it? Perhaps I can be of assistance."

Eva lit a cigarette and blew the smoke out slowly. She said, "The Americans appear to be following your guidelines. Our radar shows no aircraft in the area, as you ordered, and from what Imura reports, the American team is making itself ready to enter the area. I—I just—"

"You just what, Ms. Schmidt?" asked Fisal impatiently.

"We're still receiving erratic readings from our sensors in the southeast quadrant; or at least, I think they are erratic. I can't be sure."

Fisal had been made aware of the problem with the sensors in that area, but, like Mueller, he had disregarded that route as a possible entrance due to the terrain and the difficulty of movement. Besides, the Americans would have no way of knowing that they were having problems with their equipment. Still, the woman might have a point. Just because Johnson and his team were under the watchful eye of Imura did not mean that they would not attempt to sneak another team in behind him. "Come, let us contact Major Ruiz. He and his Gold Team are only a short distance from that area. We can have him make a sweep through there. I believe that will put us both at ease. Then I must contact the

Americans and ask about their hesitancy, and what has caused their delay."

1030 hours
Johnson's Team

B.J. whispered for a halt. Fisal was on the radio. Johnson knelt down next to Mattson and listened as Fisal demanded to know what was causing the delay. Hayes's voice came back, following the preplanned script. There were reports of armed civilians trying to sneak into the area somewhere to the north. They were trying to remove them from the area. They wanted no mistakes. It would take another hour to locate them and place them under arrest. Fisal paused, then reminded Hayes of the time limit and the explosives. The timer had been activated. With a certain air of confidence, Hayes calmly replied that they were not worried about that. Once they began the game, SOCOM would move through Fisal's troops with plenty of time to spare. Fisal had acknowledged the confidence, and said he would be waiting. Then he went off the air.

"Boy, that ol' man Hayes sure knows how to deal out the bullshit, doesn't he?" said B.J.

Johnson laughed. "It's a fine art, my boy. One that must be perfected to the nth degree if you ever want to run the CIA. Let's get going. Hayes just bought us another hour. Let's make good use of it."

B.J. swung the heavy radio back upon his broad shoulders and signaled for Johnny and Jake to move out. According to Johnny's calculations, by using the trail, they had saved time and were already halfway to the terrorist camp. They were ahead of schedule. It was welcome news that rekindled a fire in the weary men.

• • •

Major Ruiz cursed under his breath as he swung the machete down, cutting off the head of the poisonous coral snake whose gleaming, banded body curled and twisted in the noonday sun. He hated this godforsaken place and couldn't wait to return to Cuba. He was tired of the snakes, the spiders, the finger-long scorpions, and the damn alligators. Why the Americans had ever wanted to take this place from the Indians was beyond comprehension. Up ahead, Captain Garcia raised his hand and halted the nine-man team. Ruiz moved up to where his junior officer was kneeling to check a boot print in the dirt.

"What is it, Captain?" asked the major.

Garcia was silent for a moment. His dark eyes strained to search the lush green of the thick grass and trees around them. "This is a fresh track, Major. Made by a jungle boot."

"It could be Herr Mueller's. They were out here yesterday checking the sensors."

"No, sir. Mueller and his people wear German-made bush boots. This is an American jungle boot. And see, over there, near the edge of the trail, two more sets, all different sizes. Someone has been through here, Major—and not very long ago, either," said Garcia nervously, as he stood, flipped the safety off his rifle, and slowly turned, searching the brush for anything out of the ordinary. Garcia's actions alerted the others. They, too, flipped their weapons to the ready position and slowly crouched down, facing left and right into the bushes. There was a strange silence that hung in the air.

Ruiz unfastened the radio handset from his web gear and brought it up to his mouth. He felt a sudden urgency to report this to Fisal. He never got the chance. The steel bolt from Johnny's crossbow sliced through the air, striking the earpiece of the handset. It shattered the plastic and passed straight through Major Ruiz's head.

Everything seemed to happen at the same time. B.J. kicked Garcia's gun from his hands, while at the same time he swung a razor sharp bowie knife to his right and cut another man's throat to the spine. Jake and Tommy both leaped out of the bush at the same time. They slapped the weapons of two men down and buried their knives to the hilt in the chests of both men. Johnson swung his rifle down, knocking a weapon from the man in front of him. He brought the butt of his rifle up, catching the startled man a solid blow under the chin, snapping his head back with such force that it broke his neck. Using his hulking size, Hatch jumped on two men, kicked their weapons aside, gripped both by their collars, and slammed their heads together, letting them drop to the ground. Taking the knife from between his teeth, he fell on them and cut their throats.

Another bolt flew, striking another man in the forehead and dropping him like a dead bull. Garcia was groping to pull his pistol from its shoulder holster. B.J. had just dispatched another Cuban when he turned and saw Garcia. Their eyes met for a split second. B.J. recognized him as the man who had given him the tape at Gadsden Point. Garcia appeared shocked to see Mattson. It wasn't supposed to have happened this way.

Flipping the big knife in his hand, B.J. held the tip of the blade, brought his arm back and threw it as hard as he could. The blade went straight through Garcia's hand and sliced the young Cuban officer's heart in half. Death was instant.

The swamp was silent again. Not a shot had been fired. Working swiftly, the men pulled the bodies off the trail and into the bushes, where they were covered with palms and saw grass. Johnny grabbed a tree branch and began brushing over the blood and wiping away any trace of the deadly battle that had taken place. Tossing the limb off to the side, he loaded another bolt in his crossbow and hustled up to the front to take the point again. There was no talking. There was nothing to say. They had merely done what they came to do. There were no rules, and the killing had just begun.

CHAPTER 12

1300 hours
Terrorist Base Camp

Ahmad Fisal's tone was demanding. He wanted answers, and he wanted them now. Why was the American team stalling? Didn't they know that they had already lost precious time? They had only to look upon the unfortunate men hanging from the trees in front of them to erase any doubt that he would kill the hostages. The game must begin—and it must begin now!

CIA Director Hayes stared anxiously at his watch. The SOCOM team had been on the ground for eight hours, but there was no way of knowing how close they were to Fisal's camp and the hostages. Fisal had already countered their ploy about armed civilians entering the area. After hours of monitoring, Fisal's sensors had not detected the supposed violation. It was clear to Hayes that the terrorist leader was becoming suspicious, as was the press. The slow strangulation of Marcus Taylor was fully documented in living color. Somber-faced news personnel stared into cameras and eulogized the poor soul while repeatedly showing the man's final moments as he struggled and gasped for air. It was shown so many times, in fact, that it had become boring. The press needed a new area in which to focus their attention. They directed that attention back to the team that was still in plain view at the edge of the swamp. Now the press was asking, "Why are they still waiting? When are they going in?" Even more disturbing to Hayes were the self-styled theories of some of the reporters. One in particular had come surprisingly close in his analysis of the reason for the delay. While on the air, live, the man stated that this could possibly be a stalling tactic to allow time for another team or series of teams to infiltrate at other points while holding Fisal's attention to the southwest. How did they know that the six men they had been showing from a distance all day were actually General J. J. Johnson and his crack team of special personnel? No one had actually shown them close up before they appeared in the field beyond the highway, and so far, none of them had turned toward the cameras for more than a fleeting second or two. Just who were the six men in jungle fatigues and combat gear who seemed so hesitant to begin Fisal's game?

The report made Hayes livid with rage. He wanted to jerk the damn newsman up by the neck, drag him off behind one of the news vans, and ask him if it was true that ultrasound could shrink hemorrhoids—then, shove that microphone up the idiot's ass to find out. Hayes had nothing against the freedom of the press, but total ignorance was something else.

Fisal's patience had run out. Keying his mike, he told Hayes that Johnson and the others had thirty minutes to begin the game or he would begin eliminating the hostages, one every ten minutes. This would continue until he received a report from his people that the Americans had entered the area, and the game had begun.

Going to their second plan, Hayes offered the Arab leader

the opportunity to do a personal interview via radio with the top news agencies that were present. They had misjudged the Arab's personal ego. Fisal refused the offer. He would begin the executions at 2:00 P.M., with another every ten minutes until his demands were met. The radio went silent. A man who had dealt with more than a few nasty situations in his lifetime, Hayes was visibly shaken by the abrupt turn of events. His outrage was fired more by his total inability to do anything to stop the terrorist leader from carrying out his threat. Everything now depended on Johnson and his team. Hayes looked at his watch. The first hostage would die in forty minutes.

Fisal turned to Eva Schmidt and asked, "How long has it been since we last heard from Major Ruiz?"

"Over two hours," replied the German Amazon. "I do not like this, Fisal. From the reports you furnished us, those men of the Special Operations Command are not known for their patience in dealing with situations of this type. I would have expected them to advance at first light, not tarry away their time waiting for clearances or approval. I fear we may have waited too long as it is."

There was little love lost between the Arab leader and this woman, but she did have a valid point. What were they really waiting for? Each tick of the clock brought the hostages closer to certain death. Where was Ruiz? As a highly competent officer, which he was, he should have called in by now. The woman was correct. Something was wrong. Grabbing up his AK-47, Fisal headed for the door. Looking back over his shoulder, he told Eva, "Contact Mueller. Have him return here with his team. Then contact Imura. Tell him that if the Americans he has under surveillance have not moved into the area by 1400 hours, he is to return here immediately. I am taking a team out to look around. You are in charge until Mueller arrives. I will leave eight of the Palestinians here with you."

Eva already held the mike in her hand as she asked, "What about the hostage executions that are to begin at ten-minute intervals? Do we still carry them out?"

"Yes," answered Fisal. "You select the first three. I do not believe we will need more than that. Begin the executions at exactly 1400 hours. Are there any other questions?"

Eva flashed a sadistic smile and shook her head no. Fisal went outside, began shouting orders, and formed a team to conduct a search for Ruiz. Receiving confirmation of Fisal's messages from both Mueller and Imura, Eva replaced the mike and went to the doorway. Leaning against the frame, she gazed out across the pen holding the hostages, as she silently began making her selections, much like a chicken hawk hovering over a henhouse. Her eyes settled on a group of teenagers clustered in one corner of the stockade. Her thoughts went back to the young girl and the teenage boys that Fisal had brought to the camp. They were an arrogant lot, these spoiled American teenagers. Time they learned of the real world. She would begin with one of them, preferably a girl.

Johnny signaled, then dropped straight down to the ground. The team did the same. There was the sound of breaking brush and distant Arabic voices. Jake held his breath as the line of men passed through the trees less than ten yards to his right. Behind him, B.J. and the others lay perfectly still. Their sweat-drenched shirts clung to their backs, their fingers were on triggers, and their thumbs on selector switches ready to flip the weapons off safe should a firefight erupt.

The voices faded, as the group headed south, in the same

direction the Cuban team had been heading earlier. Allowing the Arabs sufficient time to clear the area, Johnson sat up and motioned for the team to gather around him. Quietly, he whispered, "Okay, boys, my Arabic isn't what it should be, but from what little I overheard, that patrol is looking for the Cubans we took out back there. I figure we've got thirty, maybe forty minutes before they find the bodies; then all hell is going to break loose. Johnny, how far do you figure we are from that base camp?"

The big Seminole studied the terrain around them, then answered, "Twenty, perhaps, thirty minutes, if we pick up the pace."

The general raised the Velcro covering the face of his watch. It was 1:45 P.M. "Okay, we'll have to pick up the pace. We have to be at that camp before that patrol radios back that they have found the bodies of the Cubans." Turning to Hatch, Johnson said, "Erin, you and B.J. have only one purpose in life when we reach that camp—locate the timer and main detonator connecting that C-4. If they have time to trigger those explosives, everybody dies."

There was a moment of silence. It was something no one wanted to think about, but yet, it was a raw reality.

"Jake," continued Johnson, "you and Johnny will go for the main gate. Blow the lock and get in there as quickly as you can. Try to get the hostages rounded up and keep them down. The rest of us will take them on outside the fence. You and Johnny do what you can from the inside, but no matter what, don't leave those people alone in there. Got it?"

"Roger, sir," replied Jake. "We've got it."

"This is it, then. From here on out, we make it up as we go along," said the general. "Good luck and may God help us. Let's hit it. We've got some pretty scared people in there who are expecting us."

1355 hours
The Stockade

Three of the Palestinians walked through the gate with Eva
Schmidt. The hostages were all on their feet as the blond
woman and her escort strolled slowly toward the teenagers
grouped together in the corner. Helen, Nancy, and Charlotte
all moved out to the center of the square. "I wonder what
they're up to now?" said Nancy.

Charlotte felt an uneasy feeling grip her stomach. There
was something about the look on the German's face.
Humorous, yet threatening. "I don't know, Nancy, but it
can't be anything good."

Jason Mattson whispered to his friend, Troy, "Let's get
Angela and Amber out of here and over to our moms."

Troy nodded and took Amber's hand. "Come on, sis, you
and Angela come with us."

The girls were frightened. Each felt the cold stare of the
approaching woman on them. Angela clasped her brother's
hand tightly. Jason could feel her trembling. "It'll be okay,
sis, just stay close to me."

The four kids moved only a few feet when Eva barked,
"Where do you think you're going? I gave no one permis-
sion to move."

Jason and Troy both ignored the woman and pulled their
sisters forward. "Halt, you obstinate little bastards!" Turning to her escort, she said, "Bring those two girls."

The Palestinians stepped forward and reached for the
girls. Troy Smith kicked one in the groin and brought his
cupped hands down on the head of the man as he doubled
over from the pain. A rifle butt shot out rapidly, catching
the boy on the side of the jaw and knocking him off his feet.
Grabbing the barrel of the rifle, Jason yelled for the girls to

run and delivered a solid punch to the jaw of the Palestinian who had hit Troy, but it was a futile effort. The remaining two guards stepped forward and beat Jason to the ground with their rifle butts.

Reaching out, Eva grabbed Angela Mattson by the hair and jerked her off her feet. Terrified, the girl screamed out in pain. Charlotte screamed as well, and ran toward her daughter and son, followed closely by Nancy and the entire camp of hostages. "Let her go, you goddamn bitch," yelled Charlotte as she tore into Eva Schmidt with both hands flying.

"Get this whore off me," shouted Eva, as she fought to pull away from the outraged mother. A guard threw his arm around Charlotte's neck. Half choking her, he pulled her away from Eva. Raising a hand to her face, Schmidt winced as she touched the deep scratches on her cheek. Pulling her hand away and seeing the blood on her fingertips, she pulled a pistol and stepped up to the struggling woman. Placing the weapon at the side of Charlotte's head, she cocked the hammer back. "I should kill you right now, bitch!" screamed Eva.

"Do it, then, damn you! But don't you touch my kids again, you pitiful excuse for a human being! Go ahead! Your time will be coming soon enough, slut! Their father will blow your damn brains all over this fence when he gets here. So, you do whatever you want for now, but you're dead already, you just don't know it yet."

Eva tightened the tension on the trigger, then hesitated. Grinning, she lowered the pistol. "So, we were fortunate enough to net the whore and the children of one of the mighty heroes of the SOCOM command. That is very interesting information. As the general is too old, and the navy stud is single, then that would make you the cow of Major Mattson, correct?"

Charlotte stopped struggling, but did not answer.

"Of course, the great B. J. Mattson. Tell me, Mrs. Mattson, have you ever screwed his partner, Commander Mortimer? I hear he is quite the stud with the ladies. Never mind, it does not matter. I will not kill you, Mrs. Mattson. That would be too simple and over too quickly." Eva paused. Stepping over to Angela, who sat crying with her hands clasped tightly over her eyes, Eva ran her fingers through the young girl's long blond hair. "No, I think I would rather watch your face as we execute this one. Take her!" ordered Eva.

"No! No!" screamed Charlotte, renewing her struggle to free herself from the Palestinian's grip. Angela screamed, "Momma! Momma! Help me!"

The whole camp was in an uproar, as the guards pulled the young girl toward the gate. Nancy and her daughter knelt on the ground, attending to Troy. Eva stepped forward and looked down at the young girl. "You are her friend. You will be next."

"Like hell, she will," screamed Nancy, leaping to her feet. Eva was ready this time. Sidestepping the woman's clenched fist, Eva brought her knee up into the pit of Nancy's stomach. Air gushed out of her as she doubled over. Schmidt brought the barrel of her pistol down solidly on Nancy's head, knocking her unconscious. Charlotte went limp in the man's arms. She had fainted. Releasing her, he let her fall to the ground. Jason, his face a bloody mess, crawled over to his mother and shielded her with his body.

As Eva turned to leave, Helen Cantrell screamed, "How, in God's name, can you justify the killing of children?"

Eva laughed. "I have killed many children much younger than these two. There is little in this life that I have not done. I am not a whining old woman like so many of you."

"Please," begged Helen, "let the girl go. We have done everything that you have asked. Don't do this thing, please."

"Enough of this whining," huffed Eva. "I am already behind schedule. I was to have executed one of you ten minutes ago. Fisal is not an understanding man in such matters. Now, out of my way."

"I know one thing that you have never done, fräulein!" said a voice from the rear of the crowd. It was a man's voice.

The hostages stepped aside, and Eva found herself staring at the little man with the purple shirt and Bermuda shorts.

"And just what would that be, little man?"

For the first time in his life, Sweet spoke without hesitation and without concern for himself, "I'm willing to bet that you have never personally executed an American general."

Helen brought her hand up to her mouth in shock as Eva grinned and replied, "That is true, little man. That would be quite an accomplishment, indeed. Perhaps, one day I will have that chance."

With steadfast determination, Raymond Sweet took three steps toward Schmidt. Reaching into his shirt pocket, he removed his military ID card and handed it to the woman. "Today is your lucky day, fräulein; General Raymond T. Sweet, Deputy Commander of SOCOM, at your service."

Eva took the card. A look of doubt as to the man's claim clearly showed in her eyes. Looking at the rank designation and the picture on the ID, she muttered, "Well, I'll be damned; you were not kidding. You are a general."

"Yes, I am," replied Sweet with a tone of pride. "And I request that you allow me to take that young lady's place. If you have to shoot someone, then why not an American general? Not some sixteen-year-old girl."

Silence fell over the crowd as the woman considered the offer. Sweet, standing steel-rod straight and with unblinking eyes, awaited Eva's decision. The novelty of the idea excited her. Sure, why not? "As you wish, General," said Eva. Waving for the guards to bring the girl back inside the wire, she looked at Sweet and asked, "Will my men have to escort you outside the wire, General?"

"Not at all, madam. I have made my decision alone. I will walk out alone."

Angela came running and dropped down into her mother's waiting arms. Looking up with tears flowing down her cheeks, Charlotte said, "General Sweet, I—" Sweet raised his hand to quiet her. "No, Mrs. Mattson, you don't have to say anything. You made me realize a number of things last night when you spoke so highly of your husband and the others of this command. I now realize I have misjudged them terribly. For enlightening me to that fact, I thank you, and I wish you all well." Touching Angela softly on the head, Sweet turned, and in perfect military fashion walked out the gate. Eva and the Palestinians followed closely behind.

A solemn silence hung over the hostages as Sweet was escorted to the base of a large cypress tree ten yards from the wire. His hands were tied behind his back and a blindfold was offered, which the little man, who had suddenly become a giant in the eyes of the hostages, politely refused. Backing him up against the tree, the guards stepped out of the line of fire as Eva Schmidt let the bolt of her AK-47 go forward, locking a round in the chamber. Sweet found himself remarkably calm as he watched the preparations for his death. His had not been a remarkable career; he knew that. He had always tried, but realized he was a total failure as an officer. He made too many mistakes and had only reached this high status through scheming and back-room politics. He held the title; but in his heart, he had always known that he did not possess the greatness that made men like General Johnson, Mattson, and Mortimer. He had always envied those men the loyalty and respect shown by the men under their command. It was a respect that he had never known.

As Eva raised her rifle, Sweet cast one last glance at the faces along the wire. His eyes came to rest on the girl called Angela as she stood huddled in her mother's embrace. Her face was turned away from what was about to happen. Maybe, just maybe, he had finally earned a small degree of respect.

The shot tore through Sweet's chest, slamming him hard against the base of the tree. A burning fire gripped his lungs as he slowly slid to the ground. A trail of blood followed his slow decline. The burning stopped. His eyes began to glaze over, but not before a small smile etched its way across his dying face. In the final seconds of his life, before everything went dark, Sweet saw justice in the form of snow-white hair, as General Johnson stepped from the trees directly behind Eva.

The need for silence no longer needed, Johnson yelled, "You fucking bitch!"

Eva, startled, turned and stared directly into the barrel of the MP5 Johnson held leveled at her chest. She made a desperate attempt to bring up her own rifle. She didn't make it. The general stitched her with a burst that went from her left kneecap to her right eye, tearing her apart.

Explosions and gunfire erupted all around the small camp as Hatch and B.J. split off in separate directions and raced around the perimeter of the stockade in search of the primary detonator and the timer. Jason and Troy both realized what was happening and what B.J. was looking for. Jumping to their feet and running at a crouch, they hurried toward the wire. They had watched the terrorists plant the charges and had seen where they had tied in the main wires. "Dad! Dad!" yelled Jason, waving frantically. "Over here! Here, by the gate!"

B.J. cut loose with a long burst that took one of the Palestinians off his feet. Running past the wounded man, B.J. squeezed off three more rounds, blowing the man's head apart. Seeing the boys waving and yelling, he screamed for them to get down. He broke for the spot they were pointing to. Tossing his rifle to the side, Mattson furiously scooped the dirt aside, and dug for the detonator. At the same instant, Jake and Johnny rushed past him, blew the lock on the gate, and ran inside, screaming for all the people to join them in the far corner of the stockade. It was not an order that had to be repeated twice.

A Palestinian found cover behind a tree and sighted in on B.J.'s back. From across the compound, Tommy Smith shouldered the big .50 caliber weapon. He could only see the barrel of the target's gun sticking out from behind the tree. He hoped Hayes hadn't exaggerated about the effectiveness of this cannon.

Centering the sight in the middle of the tree, Tommy fired. The huge slug slammed into the tree, going straight through the wood like a hot knife through butter, and literally cut the Palestinian in half. "Goddamn!" yelled Tommy. "The damn thing really works!"

Hatch scrambled around the wire, dropped down beside Mattson, and began to dig. They felt the plastic and the box at the same time. B.J. pulled it free and tore the wires loose as a hail of bullets tore across the pile of dirt next to him. Hatch moaned, then straightened up on his knees. His hands were clutching his chest. Blood oozed between his fingers.

B.J. looked up into the big man's eyes as Hatch whispered, "Ain't this a fuckin' shame!" He pitched forward into the dirt. Hatch was dead.

Kurt Mueller and his team increased their fire as they moved toward the camp. The German saw movement to his right. He brought his weapon up to fire, then he stopped. It was Fisal.

"How many are there?" yelled the Arab.

"I don't know," screamed Mueller, trying to be heard over the roar of automatic weapons fire. "Move your people in from the right. I'll go left. We'll get them in a cross fire." Fisal signaled his approval of the idea and moved off to the right. Mueller motioned his men left.

B.J. had crawled back toward the moat that surrounded the stockade. He was reloading when Tommy Smith dashed by carrying an armful of weapons that he had taken from the dead Palestinians. Running along the fence, he stopped near Jake and tossed them over the wire. The six male hostages inside scrambled for the guns, loaded them, and began to fire alongside Jake and the Seminole. The entire camp was now a hotbed of flying lead and dying men. Terrified women and children clung to the ground. Some were crying; others prayed.

Seeing Mueller's flanking movement to the left, Jake waved to B.J. and made a circling motion with his finger. Mattson nodded that he understood and slid off into the water of the moat. Moving slowly through the water, he peered over the embankment and saw Mueller and his people twenty yards ahead of him. Easing himself out of the water, he crawled into the trees and circled around behind the German. Meanwhile, Jake and two of the men moved to a point along the wire where he expected Mueller to come out of the woods. The moat had been a good idea for containing the hostages, but now it would prove a hindrance to the very men who had built it.

Mueller gave the signal, and his men rushed forward, firing as they ran. Jake waited until they were at the edge of the water, then he shouted, "Let 'em have it!"

The oncoming line of men ran straight into a wall of steel. The line wavered, then collapsed, as bullets tore through muscle and bone. Men died screaming, or they silently tumbled into the dirty water. The few who had not been hit in the initial bursts from Jake and his men turned to run back to the safety of the trees, only to run headlong into B.J., who cut them down one at a time, until all that remained of Mueller's forces were scattered bodies and moaning wounded.

Slamming a fresh magazine into his rifle, Mattson moved up the moat to make sure that no terrorists were hiding in the ditch. As he looked over the rim, he saw Mueller lying against the bank. Both of his arms had been shattered by bullets. A gleaming white bone protruded just below the shoulder of his right arm. Four other men floated facedown in the water around the German, who looked up at B.J. through pain-ridden eyes. He recognized Mattson from the photo in his file. Mueller's rifle lay only a few inches away, but it would do him no good. His arms were no more than deadweights hanging from his body.

"I told Fisal he could not trust you Americans to play stupid games by the rules," said Mueller bitterly.

"I didn't think you people had any rules, Mueller," replied Mattson dryly.

"I am a soldier, just as you are, Major Mattson. I am not a cold-blooded killer like these others. Surely, that alone entitles me to some rights of the soldier's code."

B.J. felt he was going to be sick at any minute. Having scum like this compare himself to true soldiers and the honored code was sickening. Mattson shook his head sadly as he turned to walk away.

"Mattson, wait a minute. Mattson. Can you get me a medic? The pain is terrible," said Mueller, confident that he had deterred the American's plan of killing him.

Turning back to the terrorist, B.J. said, "You'll have to wait until this is over, Mueller. We're kind of busy right now. If you're still alive when it's finished, I'll get a medic."

"That is all right, my friend. We Germans are a strong race. I will be alive and waiting for you to return."

"Sounds fair to me, Mueller," said B.J. as he turned and took two steps from the moat. Mueller was still smiling to himself, when he heard a ping sound come from somewhere in front of Mattson, who said, "This one's on General Sweet, asshole."

Mueller watched with terror-stricken eyes as Mattson flipped his hand backward. The grenade arched high into the air. It landed on the bank and rolled downward, stopping only inches from Mueller's head. "Mattson! No!" The explosion ended the need for any further conversation.

Fisal had waited for Mueller to start his attack so that it might divert attention away from him and his Palestinians. However, Johnson and Smith had not fallen for the trick. Instead, they had waited until Fisal had moved into the open, then they caught the terrorist in a deadly cross fire, wiping out all but Fisal and one remaining Palestinian soldier. No longer was the Arab thinking of a holy victory. Escape now became a primary concern, but which way were they to go? The Americans seemed to be everywhere at once, and Fisal had only one man left to use as a decoy. Tapping the man on the shoulder, Fisal pointed to the left and told the man to run; he would cover him. Apprehensive but obedient, the soldier did as he was told. On his feet and running, the man made it to the trees. He waved for Fisal to follow. Suddenly, the tree seemed to explode and the upper half of the man's chest was ripped open. Smith was getting pretty good with that dinosaur rifle.

Fisal was sweating heavily as another round from the fifty tore a chunk of dirt the size of a basketball from the ground next to him. Where had the plan gone wrong? He had worked every detail out with Ruiz, Mueller, and Imura—Imura! Where was the Japanese and his people? As if on cue, the little Oriental and the Avenging Sun charged out of the trees. They opened fire on the people in the stockade. It was the diversion Fisal had been praying for. Peering from behind his tree, the Arab watched the Oriental terrorist mount a suicidal frontal attack against the Americans. It was a foolish move. Within minutes, they found themselves in a devastating cross fire and were dropping like flies. Imura was hit twice before he fell to the ground. His ever-faithful mistresses knelt at his side until they, too, were cut to pieces by the deadly, accurate fire of the Americans.

The smell of cordite and thick, drifting clouds of gunsmoke slowly drifted away as quiet fell over the battleground. No one noticed the lone figure crawling away in the shadows.

Slowly, cautiously, B.J. and the others stood. Their weapons were still at the ready. They told the civilians to stay down and began a careful sweep of the camp.

Moving to Fisal's headquarters, Johnson and Jake flanked the doorway while B.J. kicked the door open. He and Johnny burst inside. It was empty. Johnson entered and immediately heard a familiar voice coming over the radio in the corner. It was Will Hayes. He was trying to contact Fisal.

Placing his rifle on a chair, he picked up the mike, and in a relieved but tired voice, he said, "Will, this is Johnson. It's all over. Get me some medical personnel and choppers in here ASAP! We can use the hostage containment area to land the choppers. I'll have it marked for them. I don't want to see any damn press people on those choppers, Will! You got that?"

Hayes sounded as relieved as Johnson. "Loud and clear, Jonathan. Did you get Fisal?"

"No, the bastard got away, somehow, but I have a feeling we haven't seen the last of that boy. You can count on it. Get those choppers in here right away, Will."

"On the way! Out."

Taking his rifle, General J. J. Johnson joined the others for the walk up the hill to the smiling, crying faces of those who had never lost faith in them. Along the way, they stopped and solemnly saluted a fallen comrade, General Raymond Sweet, who, in the end, had proven that he was as good a man as any of them. At last he had become a member of the team.

As they crossed the bridge and entered the stockade, wild cheers of happiness resounded as families were reunited, and prayers echoed. Helen ran to Johnson and fell unashamed into the general's arms, hugging him tightly. Jake was led to where Beverly Mills sat crying hysterically. He knelt down and held her to him as he tenderly whispered, "It's all right, Bev. I'll take care of you from now on. No one will ever hurt you again. I promise."

As the choppers approached in the distance, B.J. wrapped his arm around Charlotte's waist and asked, "Are you ready to go home for good this time?"

Holding her kids close to her, Charlotte managed a smile as she said, "Yes we are, Colonel, but, if you don't mind, I think we'll forgo any more promotion celebrations."

CONFIRMED KILL

They're the antiterrorist team of the future—stepping across the law to crush the criminals of tomorrow.

Con Duggan is the shooter with nerves of steel; techno-wizard Steve Dye keeps them both alive. They carry the 21st century's most secret weapon, the SIKIM 1000 multiple-delivery killing tool. They answer only to the President . . .

And they don't take prisoners.

Turn the page
for an excerpt from this exciting
new action/adventure series
from Diamond Books.

"Penelope! I'm going to shoot at the *Stingray*! Get the TAD round and the barrel for it out of that gray bag!" He didn't have to tell her twice. She scrambled around the deck as lead smacked against the old bus like a thousand heavy stones. The bus shuddered and the remaining glass shattered. Light everywhere. Something whispered by his cheek, something else slipped through his leather jacket, the tug of an impatient lead child, anxious to be on its way. A thin but not fatal line of blood, no worse than a paper cut, marked its passage across his chest.

He began to return fire, this time full auto, and the tough little .40mm began to slap against the *Stingray*. He sprayed the lower decks, left to right, right to left, chewing and chipping up everything above the waterline. The boat was clear in his sighting system, alive with targets. He kept the trigger depressed until the boat shuddered to a halt, its engine running, but its rudder shot away. The *Stingray* began to go around in circles, its decks a shambles of downed men and silent guns. Steven could see one man clearly, standing in a shattered window, manning what seemed to be the last operational machine gun.

"Penelope?"

"Right here, Steven Yank."

"Hand me that barrel, and the tool that's strapped to it."

Calmly, but speedily, Steven Dye removed the hot .40mm barrel and tossed it clattering across the bus deck floor. He snapped the larger, much heavier TAD barrel on in seconds. TAD—thermal acceleration device. Half the time, it didn't work.

Steven could feel Penelope's shoulder against his as he inserted the heavy TAD round into the breech of the new barrel and powered up the scope for a TAD shot readout. He glanced at Penelope, but she paid him no attention, her eyes fixed on the *Stingray* as it circled helplessly in the harbor. Every time it got into position, the one machine gun would open up again, lead singing through the cemetery and holing the bus, miraculously turning it to junk without killing them.

The *Stingray* readout clicked through the shot computer in 14.5 seconds, printed its data and held. The scope went blue and the heat from the gun on the boat and its one-man crew pulsed a steady yellow light, shifting numbers to the side as the boat circled.

Steven Dye was positive the lone gunman on the bridge was Peter Coy Booker. The scope readout locked on the *Stingray*, selecting an aim point automatically. The scope face turned red, and a green range and speed printed a series of numbers from 2800 yards to 2841 yards. Steven switched on the pack, transferring selection bar from ready to fire optimum, or FO on the receiver switch panel, which contained three switches. FM for fire manual, SS for sightless shot, meaning no scope. In the FO, or fire optimum mode, the scope, in effect, did the shooting. For him, at the most perfect time, the TAD whooshed away at the optimum selected range of 2870 yards. It struck the

Stingray directly amidships, under Booker and his gun. It struck the section of the *Stingray* made almost exclusively of wood. A fire of awesome proportions erupted along the full length of the *Stingray*, and then, as it met an onrushing rupture from a fuel tank, the *Stingray* seemed to vanish inside a white-hot ball of flame. In less than 15 seconds, it was gone without a flicker. From 21A, circling 40,000 feet overhead, someone said, "Holy shit!"

Con Duggan glassed the harbor for a trace of the *Stingray*, but he couldn't find one. The TAD round, unpredictable most of the time, had applied more heat in one small place than any other weapon ever developed. They had done it. Peter Coy Booker was dead.

"21A?"

"Yeah, Mr. Duggan."

"Where is Rose One?"

"Still in the station, Mr. Duggan."

"Good. You can set her down now. We'll let the Brits clean up the mess. Michael says we're going home."

"All right!! 21A out."

"We did it, didn't we, Steven Yank?"

"Yup. We did it. Nobody got out of that. The damn gun really surprised me."

"Oh, why?"

"It worked, that's why. I wasn't sure it would."

Penelope walked around the bus, though hopped was a more apt description. A machine-gun slug had shot off one of her high heels.

"Oh, Steven, it will never zoom, zoom again." She sounded genuinely sad as she walked to him. "Now, Steven Yank, you must honor your promise, and take me with you to the United States."

"Did I promise that? When? When did I say that?" His face was blackened like a coal miner's from powder residue. He pulled her to him, until she wiped the grin off his face by trying to swallow his tongue with her own.

"How sweet. I hate to break this up, but I'm taking the weapon. Unfortunately, I can't allow you to live." Madeline stood in what was left of the bus's doorway, gun in hand.

Penelope broke free from Steven, tripping on her heelless shoe, falling down.

21A had been only half right. Rose One, the listening device, was still in the police station, but the wrong agent was wearing it. Maddy raised the Browning .9mm, and pointed it at Steven Dye.

"I would like to have fucked you both before you left for the States. Now, of course, you won't be leaving. Stand clear of the gun."

Nine hundred yards away, Con Duggan could hear everything Maddy said. Steven Dye's communicator was open. He had neglected to close it during the battle with the *Stingray*.

Con centered the Springfield's cross hairs on Madeline, who was standing erect and starkly outlined, her gun hand extended toward Steven Dye. He could see her sleek shape, so feminine, and yet so dangerous. As he slowly tightened his finger on the trigger, the figure in the cross hairs wavered, fogged, reappeared, this time holding a child, not a gun. Sweat beaded his forehead, his mouth dry and tasting of dust and forests and blood. The figure in the scope wavered back and forth from a woman with a gun to a woman seeming to hold a child. The next time the figure appeared to hold a gun, he ended the Folkstone contract by sending a 200-grain Columbia bullet, identical to the last one he'd fired in Southeast Asia, roaring out across the cemetery and crashing into Maddy's brain.